One More

SHAMELESS NIGHT

Kidnapped by the Billionaire
Book Three

By Lili Valente

One More

SHAMELESS NIGHT

By Lili Valente

Self Taught Ninja Press

Table of Contents

About the Book

Warning: This book is one fast and furious, danger-laced, HOT as hell Happily Ever After. Come along with Harley and Clay for One More Shameless night.

Clay Hart may not work for the CIA anymore, but he has all the shady connections he needs to make sure no one f*&ks with his family. He'll be keeping a close eye on his wife, son, and newborn baby to make sure their trip to visit Harley's sister goes off without a hitch.

It's been a year since the party that almost ended Harley's life, but when her sister offers to babysit so that she and Clay can attend a Midsummer soiree, Harley jumps at the chance. What better way to put dark memories behind her than with a steamy date night with her hot as hell husband?

But old enemies are lurking in the shadows, just waiting for the Hart family to drop their guard.

Will Harley and Clay live to see the midsummer sun rise?

Or will their first date night after the birth of their second child be their last?

*One More Shameless Night is the final book in the Kidnapped by the Billionaire series.

Dedicated to my readers, who told me they wanted one more night.

Love you guys!

CHAPTER ONE

Harley

*T*he boys had been little angels on the chartered flight from their great aunt's house to the island of Samoa, the car rental had gone off without a hitch, and now both Jasper and baby Will were napping in the back seat as their daddy guided the car down a strip of asphalt beside the sea. A warm wind whipped through Harley's hair, sunlight glittered on the ocean, and all was right with the world.

Or as right as it could be considering she was going to be spending the next month sleeping in the guest room of a man she had put in prison.

A man who had emerged from prison to become a hardened criminal and spent the next several years of his life hunting her down with every intention of breaking her soul into tiny jagged pieces—and maybe killing her when he was finished. Jackson Hawke had been derailed before he could prove if he had it in him to go completely psycho killer on the woman who had ruined his life and destroyed his career, but if things had gone a little differently, Harley had an ugly feeling that she would be six feet under right now.

Sure, she'd apologized profusely, Jackson had accepted, and they'd all agreed to move forward, but she knew most people would consider her bat shit crazy for agreeing to spend her summer vacation at her sister's house, isolated from the world on an island with a former mortal enemy.

But for Harley, it was just another slightly dysfunctional family gathering. Nothing she wasn't used to after being raised by a psychopath and the mother he'd destroyed. She could get through this with her eyes closed and one hand tied behind her back.

Right?

Harley swallowed hard and tightened her grip on the "Oh Shit" handle above the door.

Beside her, Clay chuckled beneath his breath. "It's going to be fine," he said, reading her mind. As usual. "Stop worrying."

"But I like worrying," she said, picking at a loose thread on the car seat with her free hand. "It's not too late to get a hotel for the entire trip, you know. We already have a room for tonight and there were long-term reservations available at three different resorts and a couple of nice bed and breakfast places. I checked."

"Of course you did."

She wrinkled her nose in his direction. "If you still want to go to the party later, we could hire a sitter to watch the kids. And I bet the boys would love to swim in a pool. Pools are fun for small people."

Clay nodded. "Think Will's going to be doing a lot of swimming, do you?"

"It's never too early to start teaching kids to swim," Harley countered, not in the mood to indulge her husband's sarcastic side. "By the time he was two, Jasper could make it all the way across the lake on our old property. He was swimming like a fish way before he could read."

Clay cast an amused look her way. "Two years, babe. Not two months."

"So? I'm going to be a more proactive mom this time around." Harley lifted her chin, refusing to concede defeat. "I'm going to anticipate things. Prepare for things."

She glanced over her shoulder, making sure Jasper was still asleep before adding in a softer voice, "Things like the fact that my sister's enormous, scary husband might be planning to strangle me in my sleep and orphan my children."

"Jackson isn't going to strangle you while you sleep," Clay said, the teasing note vanishing from his tone. "He's as ready as we are to put the past behind us."

"But what if he's changed his mind?" Harley nibbled at her bottom lip as the road narrowed and the thick jungle foliage pressed in on the right side of the road, making her feel vaguely claustrophobic. "It's been over a year since you talked to him, and he wasn't overly friendly when he and I chatted on the phone. Things can change, you know. Old wounds can lose their scabs and start bleeding and pussing and oozing all over the place."

"That's a disgusting way to put it."

"Well they can," she insisted. "Stable people can become unstable again and homicidal tendencies you think have passed you by can suddenly..." She whipped her hand in a circle in front of her face. "Resurge. At a moment's notice. Probably the moment when you see the person you wanted to murder again for the first time in several years."

"I called him last night," Clay said, surprising her. "We had a long talk."

"You did?" She clenched the plastic bar in her right hand even tighter. "When?"

"After you and the boys were asleep. I needed to make sure he and I were on the same page before we got on the plane this morning." He reached out, threading his fingers through hers and squeezing tight. "When I promised I wouldn't let anyone hurt you again, I meant it. No one touches you. No one scares you. No one so much as looks at you in a way that makes you wonder if you're safe."

He brought their joined hands to his lips and pressed a kiss to the warm skin below her wedding ring. "You and the boys are the most important things in the world to me. When it comes to keeping you all around for a long, long time, I'm not taking any chances."

"I know." Harley blinked faster as unexpected tears rose in her eyes. "Hey...I love you. Have I said that today?"

"I love you, too." His smile ripped her heart to pieces and stitched it back together again. How had she lived so long without that smile? Those dancing blue eyes? This man?

"And yes," he said. "I still want to go to the party. I can't wait to be alone with you. It's all

I can think about."

"Oh, yeah?" She let her gaze slide down to his lap and lifted a wry brow. "So that's not a banana in your pocket?"

"Jasper ate all the bananas before we landed," Clay said before adding in a huskier voice. "That's why I booked a room for us tonight. So when we're done at the party, I can take you to bed, and not worry about anyone overhearing when I make you scream."

Harley's thighs pressed together, an instinctive response to the heat spreading through her pelvis though his words inspired nearly as much anxiety as desire.

It felt like forever since they'd been together. The last few weeks before Will was born, she'd been too miserable to make love—as big as a rhinoceros and twice as cranky—and her doctor had advised her to wait six-to-eight weeks after the baby's birth before having sex.

But Will had hit the two-month mark three days ago and so far he was the best baby in the world. He only got up twice a night to take a bottle and went right back to sleep as soon as his diaper was changed. He wouldn't give Hannah any trouble while Harley and Clay were gone and Jasper had been video chatting with his aunt for weeks. He was giddy with excitement for their impending sleepover. Hannah had promised that they would stay up late, light tiki torches on the patio, and watch a movie on her outdoor projector surrounded by junk food.

Harley had no doubt that her children were going to be fine…which unfortunately left more energy to stress about the evening to come.

"You're not worried about leaving Will, are you?" Clay asked, squeezing her hand again.

Harley shook her head. "No. Hannah is the nicest person in the world. Babies love her on sight. I have no doubt she'll take perfect, sweet care of Will and Jasper and they will all have a wonderful time."

"Then what's wrong?"

"I just…" She peeked into the backseat again, half hoping Jasper would be awake and give her an excuse not to tell the truth.

But the boys were both still sleeping, and she was committed to being honest with Clay as often as possible—the better to make up for the secrets she felt obligated to keep, even from the man she loved.

She turned back to him with a sigh. "I'm a little different than I was this time last year." She tugged at the bottom of her shirt, hyper aware of the saggy belly skin beneath her flowing black tank top and the silvery stretch marks Will, who had been a much bigger baby than Jasper, had left behind on her hips. "Back then, I was in the best shape of my life, not two months postpartum with dimples in gross places and—"

She cut off with a soft cry as Clay suddenly veered onto a narrow turnout on the side of the road, sending gravel flying as he braked the car.

"What's wrong?" she asked, pressing a hand to her chest. "Shit. You scared me half to death.'

Clay shoved the car into park and turned to her, cupping her face in his hands, holding her gaze with an intensity that left her feeling even more anxious and exposed.

"Stop it." The passion in his voice killed the tension-defusing joke on the tip of her tongue. "You are beautiful. Incredible. Irresistible."

Harley huffed as she rolled her eyes. "Don't push it."

"I'm not pushing anything." He leaned closer, his breath warming her lips, making her heart beat even faster. "When I look at you, I see a woman so stunning and sexy it's all I can do not to drag you off into the jungle right now and prove to you how irresistible you are."

Harley's lips parted, but before she could respond, a sleepy voice from the backseat said—

"Are we going to play Tarzan?"

As he turned to Jasper, Clay's hands shifted from her face to squeeze her shoulders, that simple touch assuring her that every word he'd said was true.

And that she was one damned lucky woman.

"Why do you ask that, buddy?" Clay asked, lips curving.

"Tarzan dragged people into the jungle," Jasper replied, making it clear he'd heard at least the tail end of their conversation. "But only bad people. Is Mama going to pretend to be the bad guy?"

"Maybe later. I like it when Mama pretends to be bad," Clay said with a straight face, earning himself a slap on the leg while Harley fought to swallow the laugh rising inside of her. "But right now we should get back on the road. Aunt Hannah and Uncle Jackson are waiting for us and Will is going to need a bottle soon. You ready?"

Jasper's yawn turned into a smile. "Yes! I can't wait to show Aunt Hannah my baby brother. She's going to go crazy over this little cutie."

Heart aching with happiness, Harley reached back to ruffle Jasper's hair. "You're pretty cute, yourself, big brother. I'm so excited to spend a month on the beach with you. We're going to have so much fun."

"Me too." Jasper grinned, mischief

flickering in his deep blue eyes. "Maybe we'll like it so much we'll decide to stay forever."

"I thought you were excited about having Mrs. Miner for first grade," Clay said, glancing over his shoulder at the road behind them.

"I'm more excited about sand," Jasper said practically. "And digging the biggest hole in the universe and boogie boarding and swimming and snorkeling and catching a giant fish and eating the whole thing all by myself."

Harley laughed. "You're a beach addict."

Jasper stretched his arms over his head and shrugged. "Better than being addicted to video games."

"Wise words from a wise little man." Clay gave Harley's thigh a final squeeze before pulling back onto the road.

As they continued along the coast toward the quiet, seaside town where Hannah and Jackson had made their home—Jasper chattering non-stop and baby Will sweetly sleeping through it all—Harley tried to relax and catch her son's excitement.

But despite the romantic speech from her husband and a heart full of love and gratitude for the two amazing kids she was lucky enough to call family, she couldn't let her guard down completely. She knew that behind the seemingly peaceful life she and Clay had built, something big and bad lurked in the shadows, threatening everything she held dear.

Now wasn't the time to relax her defenses, no matter how far they were from the man who threatened her or how safe this island seemed.

Hours later, when she was facing down yet another Midsummer moonrise with a gun to her back, she would remember the feeling and swear—if she lived through the night—never to ignore her intuition again.

LILI VALENTE

14

CHAPTER TWO

Clay

*J*ackson, his former best friend—who also used to sleep with Clay's wife seven years ago—was now his brother-in-law. He was married to Harley's twin sister, Hannah, who Jackson had mistakenly kidnapped about eighteen months ago, thinking she was Harley, and made his sex slave for a couple of months before getting around to the marriage and happily ever after bit.

No matter what Clay had said to Harley, or how reassuring Jackson had been on the phone, this situation was weird as fucking hell and a part of Clay was dreading this family get together every bit as much as Harley was.

He pulled down the gravel road leading to Jackson and Hannah's home with a lead weight forming in his stomach. By the time he parked the rental car next to a black SUV, in the shadow of a luxurious take on a typical island pole house, he had developed a full blown case of the Turn Back Nows.

What if Harley and Jackson brought out the worst in each other? What if they both refused to play nice?

He loved his wife like nothing else in the world, but playing nice wasn't always her strong suit and Jackson could put the capital S in Son of a Bitch when he was so inclined. Spending four weeks trapped in a house with an irate Jackson, a hissing and spitting Harley, a sister-in-law who was practically a stranger, and two kids under the age of eight, while they all tried to pretend to be normal people, sounded like a slice of hell on earth.

As Clay reached for the door handle, his palm was slick with sweat.

Relax. Or at least, pretend to be relaxed.

If you don't, Harley is going to see you're stressed the fuck out, and she might start to wonder if there's more than family-visit inspired jitters to blame.

The thought steadied his pulse. No matter what else happened, Harley couldn't find out what he and Jackson were up to behind the scenes. Not until it was too late to stop the boulders they'd put in motion from rolling down the hill and crushing everything in their path.

He'd meant every word he'd said to Harley in the car. She and the boys were all that mattered to him and he would go to whatever lengths necessary to protect what was his.

Even if that included taking out a hit on his lying, scheming, murder-inclined father-in-law.

"You ready for this?" Harley whispered, circling around the car to stand beside him, her shoes crunching ominously in the gravel.

He forced a smile. "I was born ready."

He had just helped Jasper out of his booster seat and unclicked Will's carrier from its base when a woman who had to be Hannah hurried around the side of the house, crying out in excitement.

"You're here! You're here," she said, her green sundress molding to her body as she shuffled across the lawn, emphasizing her incredibly pregnant belly. "You're finally here!"

A delighted squeal unlike anything Clay had ever heard emerge from his wife's lips ripped through the air, and then Harley was streaking past him, colliding with her sister in a fierce, but gentle, hug.

"A baby! You're having a baby!" Harley gasped, drawing back to touch Hannah's belly reverently before pulling her sister back into her arms and rocking her back and forth. "Oh my God, you stinker! Why didn't you tell me you were pregnant?"

"I wanted it to be a surprise. It's so rare that I have a chance to get one over on you, I couldn't resist." Hannah wiggled her fingers over Harley's shoulder. "Hi, Clay and Jasper! Welcome to our island! It's so great to finally meet you in person."

"You, too." The dread in Clay's chest began to seep away in the warmth of Hannah's sunbeam smile.

When Jackson came around the house a moment later with an easy grin on his face and pulled Clay into a similar hug—minus the squealing—the last of his worry faded away.

"We're glad to have you." Jackson pulled back, clapping him on the shoulder before shifting his gaze to the carrier in Clay's hands. He leaned down, inspecting Will's tiny face, still peaceful in sleep. "And this must be Will."

"He's my baby brother," Jasper piped up from just behind Clay. "He's eight weeks old."

"He's perfect," Jackson said, kneeling down to Jasper's level. "And you both look just like your dad. Do people tell you that all the time?"

Jasper grinned shyly. "Yes. But I've got a twisty brain like Mama's."

"Really?" Jackson lifted a wry brow. "Well,

your Mom is one of the smartest people I've ever met, so that sounds like a good combination."

"Devious might be a better word." Harley appeared on Clay's other side while Hannah rushed to hug Jasper, assuring him they were going to have a fantastic visit.

"Hello, Jackson," Harley added in a softer voice. "Thanks for having us."

Jackson's smile vanished as he stood, but his expression remained decidedly on the civil side. "Glad you could make it. Anything that makes Hannah this happy is a smart call in my book."

"You're a good husband," Harley said, proving she was also willing to play nice. "And I really do appreciate this. I can't believe I'm going to get to be here when the baby is born. With Hannah and me living so far apart I never imagined something like that would be possible."

"You're welcome." Jackson nodded before turning back to Clay with a soft clap of his hands. "All right, let's grab your suitcases. I'll carry everything in and show you where you're sleeping. We put Jasper in the guest room by ours and you and the baby in rooms on the other side of the house."

"Because we're selfish and want to sleep as much as possible before our little one arrives," Hannah said, bending down to coo over Will. "Oh, he's so beautiful, Harley! I can't wait to hold him. I need to sniff his sweet little head right now."

Harley laughed, taking the carrier from Clay. "Let's get a bottle ready first. He's a kind soul, but he can still get a banshee wail going when he's hungry."

Clay lingered near the rental car, watching the sisters and Jasper move toward the house before turning back to Jackson. "Anything new since we talked last night? Did you get the final files from the sheriff's computer?"

Jackson shook his head slightly. "No, but it's a matter of days. Maybe hours. Soon we'll have everything we need to put Stewart Mason in jail for the rest of his life. The senator will exchange his designer menswear for an orange jumpsuit and our families will be safe."

"You're sure," Clay said, trying not to get his hopes up.

He and Jackson had been working to get Harley and Hannah's father out of the picture since just after Christmas. Stewart was a threat to everything he touched and had been showing far too much interest in Jasper since Clay and Harley had returned to the States. And then, about six months ago, Clay had taken down a hit man moments before the other man's gun exploded in his face. Jackson had experienced a similar attack outside the U.S. embassy in Samoa, where he was on security detail, just a few hours later. Digging into the shooters' backgrounds in the wake of the failed assassination attempts had revealed thin, thready, but highly suspicious ties to Mason Industries.

But so far every promising lead had fizzled before Jackson and Clay discovered evidence damning enough to put Stewart away. The man was a clever monster and had done an excellent job of covering his tracks.

It made it tempting to consider taking a more direct route to solving the problem, but that avenue would remain unexplored until there was no other option. If Clay could avoid being the man who murdered his wife's father, he would prefer it.

He wanted to live the rest of his life as a good man…as soon as he made sure the people who threatened his family were somewhere they couldn't hurt anyone ever again.

"This is everything we need, wrapped up in a big bloody bow," Jackson assured him. "That bastard is going to be locked up so tight he'll never take a breath of free air again."

"Good." Clay popped the trunk and collected the larger suitcase. "I like the idea of Will never meeting his maternal grandfather."

"Same here." Jackson reached in to grab the two smaller suitcases. "Sorry about keeping the pregnancy a secret. Hannah made me promise. She was afraid you would tell Harley."

"I probably would have. I tell her everything." He slammed the trunk, following Jackson as he headed toward the house. "I'll tell her about this, too. As soon as it's too late for her to try to talk me out of it."

"Do you think she would? Harley's not exactly known for her sense of justice and fair play."

Clay's breath rushed out. "She's changed, Jackson. She really has."

"I believe you, but she hasn't changed that much." Jackson paused on the stone walkway and turned to pin Clay with a hard look. "You can't tell me a woman who loves her kids that much wants them to grow up in a world with Stewart Mason running around loose in it. Even if he hadn't tried to take us out, we know and *she* knows that he hired someone to kill his own brothers."

"Nobody's been able to prove that," Clay cautioned, feeling compelled to be the voice of reason. "Not even the CIA, and we took a long hard look at the case before he was approved for the Senate."

Jackson's gaze darkened. "It doesn't matter if there's proof. I know it's true and I'd bet my right hand my father was the one who completed the hits." His eyes rolled skyward with a sigh. "Though at this point I'll probably never know for sure. My mother isn't speaking to me. About that, or anything else."

"You and Hannah really won the grandparent lottery, didn't you?" Not for the first time, Clay felt a little guilty for having a mother and father who had always loved and supported him unconditionally, and who had embraced his wife without question simply because she made him so happy. "I could ask my parents if they want to be surrogate grandma and grandpa to baby Hawke."

Jackson shook his head. "You don't have to do that."

"I know I don't, but I'm sure they would love to. Mom always wanted a bunch of grandkids. Two is good, but three will be even better."

Jackson nodded slowly, a smile curving his lips. "Well, thank you. Hannah would love that. But you'll have to make sure they're okay with four grandkids, not three."

"Four..." Clay clapped Jackson on the shoulder with his free hand. "Oh shit, man. Twins?"

"Twins," Jackson confirmed, an uncertain expression on his usually dangerous-looking face. "Girls. Identical. The C-section is scheduled in two weeks."

Clay laughed and kept laughing until he had to put the suitcase down and press a hand to his side.

"Yeah, yeah. Laugh it up, asshole," Jackson grumbled. "But twins run in that family. You keep at it with Harley and the next time you might get more than you bargained for."

"I already did," Clay said, still laughing. "Look who I'm married to."

Jackson snorted and was soon laughing right along with him. Clay tried to regain control—knowing they should get inside—but it felt too good to laugh, to release the tension that had been haunting him since they'd started planning this trip.

Jackson and Hannah were truly happy to have them, the last enemy threatening his family would soon be behind bars, and Jackson Hawke, the alpha male to rule them all, was having twin girls.

The universe definitely had a sense of

humor.

Maybe it had a sense of justice, too, at least for those willing to help justice along. And maybe someday soon there would come a day when he wouldn't go to sleep certain that dark forces from the past were creeping in to destroy the life he'd built and the love he'd found.

As Clay followed Jackson up the steps onto the wrap around porch overlooking the ocean, he dared to imagine a future that was as wide-open and shadow free as the cloudless expanse of blue sweeping out to the horizon.

LILI VALENTE

CHAPTER THREE

The Closer

As the two men stepped inside the Hawke home The Closer sat back in the padded speedboat chair, letting the binoculars in his hand fall to dangle from his wrist.

It was finally time. Everything was ticking along right on schedule.

He'd been waiting a year for Clay and

Harley to venture outside the web of safeguards protecting them in their everyday lives. As former CIA, Clay had the best security system money could buy, ties to local and state law enforcement, and a paranoid streak a mile wide, especially since the failed shooting in January.

The man rarely let his wife or children out of his sight, and when he did, he left a tail on them, a hired gun who followed the new Mrs. Hart as she went about her daily business, protecting her from afar. And Clay himself was always carrying, packing heat beneath the mild-mannered blazer he wore to his new job as a covert operations consultant.

The Closer hadn't dared make a move on Harts' home turf. He didn't know who had sent the last man who'd tried to take Hart's life, but the speed and efficiency with which the former agent had dispatched the shooter had bred a healthy respect for the man's skills.

The Closer wasn't afraid of dying, but he was the only one left. The rest of the cartel had been killed, jailed, or scattered to the wind, never to be seen again. If Harley was going to get what was coming to her, what she deserved for betraying Marlowe, the Closer had to stay alive long enough to get the job done.

But now, the Harts were in a foreign country, and had been forced to leave their guns and goons at home. Clay and Harley were booked into the honeymoon suite at the Malolo Resort and Spa, where they would be attending tonight's Midsummer luau, and the Closer would have the chance to do what he had always done best—close the book on people who betrayed Marlowe.

Tonight was the night. It was all over but the blood and tears.

With a soft sigh that was whipped away by the ocean breeze, the Closer started the boat and set course for the other side of the island and a dock not far from the Malolo resort.

CHAPTER FOUR

Harley

*T*hree hours later, Harley stepped out onto the lanai in a stunning white dress that she'd borrowed from Hannah, a chiffon number that pushed up her boobs, swirled magically around her legs, and even more magically concealed the loose skin at her belly. Crossing to the deck railing, she cast an anxious glance onto the patio below.

There Hannah and Jasper were busy setting up for their outdoor movie while having a lively debate on the merits of chocolate covered pretzels versus chocolate covered popcorn.

Inside, Will—who had woken, charmed everyone with his gummy new smile, filled an impressively stinky diaper, taken a full eight ounces of milk, and fallen asleep again—was snoozing happily in his crib. Jackson had the baby monitor in his office, Hannah had promised to pop up and check on the baby every hour or so, they had all said their goodbyes, and Clay had gone to carry their overnight bags to the car.

She should be following him—they had nine o'clock dinner reservations in two hours and it would take them thirty minutes to get to the hotel.

But for some reason, she couldn't seem to tear herself away from the deck railing or her eyes away from Jasper. He was showing off his ninja moves, a wild display of thrashing and spinning that bore more resemblance to a spastic modern dance than karate, and was making Hannah giggle so hard she had just snorted water out of her nose.

"Everything okay?" Clay asked as he came to stand behind her, pinning her between his strong body and the railing, immediately making her feel safe and a little nervous at the same time.

"This is the first time we've left him alone with someone since last summer," she whispered, not wanting to attract Jasper's attention. He'd already made it clear he was past ready for Mom and Dad to scram so he could enjoy his movie date with Aunt Hannah. "I was worried he would be scared."

Clay wrapped his arms around her waist, pulling her back to his front. "The only thing he's scared of is you telling him he can't eat as much junk food as he wants. He's okay. He doesn't think about the kidnapping anymore. For him, all the ugliness is over."

Harley pulled in a deep breath and let it out slow and steady. "It really is. Isn't it?"

"Yes," Clay said pressing a kiss to the back of her hair. "For him and for us."

Almost she added silently, thinking of the

text she'd just received from Dom.

Big news. Call me back as soon as possible. We need to meet.

There hadn't been time to reply, or to tell him the meeting would have to wait until she was back in the States. But if her gut was right, the nightmare her father had put into motion years ago might finally be coming to an end.

And when it did, she would tell Clay the secret she'd been keeping since she woke up from a coma last year to find an email from Dom warning her that her father was on to them and that threats had been made.

Threats that involved an eye for an eye, a tooth for a tooth, and a child for a child.

If you take what's mine, I'll take what's yours, had been her father's exact words.

Meaning that if Harley kept working to find and free the half sister she'd never met, then Stewart Mason would find a way to take Jasper away from her.

And Stewart never made idle threats.

As if that wasn't bad enough, two days later, when she was still throwing off the mind-muddying effects of being unconscious for so long, she'd learned that she was pregnant.

She'd been pregnant when the helicopter crashed. Luckily, she hadn't lost the baby, but for the first several months of her pregnancy, she'd had to be careful, to keep her stress levels low and her healing on track, all while doing everything it took to make Jasper feel safe and loved. By the time she found the words to tell Clay what was going on, she couldn't bring herself to say them.

He'd been so happy, so thrilled about the baby, and so excited about the future. She couldn't ruin it, not when there was nothing he could do to make the situation better.

She couldn't back down, or tell Dom to stop trying to find Mallory. The girl didn't deserve to be imprisoned for her entire life for the sin of being Ian Hawke's daughter instead of Stewart's.

That will be a fun conversation.

Filling Jackson and Hannah in on the fact that they have a mutual half sister in common.

"You ready, beautiful?" Clay asked, taking

her hand.

"Ready." She turned to him, capturing his lips for a long, slow kiss. There would be time to sort through all the drama later.

Tonight was the shortest night of the year, the perfect time to banish all the nightmares and start fresh with the sunrise.

CHAPTER FIVE

Clay

The honeymoon hut overlooked the resort's tropical lagoon on one side and a private stretch of sugar white beach showcasing a romantically crumbling abandoned lighthouse on the other. It was far enough from the rest of the resort that the faint sounds of music and laughter from the party already in session were overshadowed by the crash of the waves and the call of hundreds of birds settling in for the night in the palm trees across the lagoon.

Inside the hut, a mosquito-net draped bed large enough to fit an entire village dominated the center of the room, his and her porcelain tubs sat facing the screen door, offering bathers a view of the lighthouse, and wicker chairs with overstuffed cushions completed the aura of comfortable elegance.

But it was the swing in the corner of the room that immediately caught Clay's eye.

The staff had installed it exactly to his specifications. As he set his and Harley's overnight bags on the floor near the bed, he made a mental note to give the concierge who'd assisted him an excellent tip. Then he turned to watch Harley, not wanting to miss the expression on her face when she saw the swing.

"This is so beautiful." She scanned the horizon, where the last of the sunset light was fading to dark blues and purples, before turning back to the room. "I love the bathtubs and the—"

She broke off, her eyes going almost comically large and her flushed cheeks paling. "Oh my God. Is that what I think it is?"

Clay grinned. "I told you I was going to get one for the house."

"The house. Not our hotel room." Harley's brow furrowed as she circled around to the far side of the room, surveying the wicker and leather creation from a different angle. "What kind of place is this, that they just happen to have a bondage swing on hand?"

"They didn't," Clay said, beginning to wonder if this had been a good idea. So far, Harley looked less than thrilled by his surprise. "It's ours. I had it made by a local wicker expert while we were in Tahiti visiting your aunt. I'd planned for it to come back to the States with us, too, but we can drag it out to the beach and burn it if you would rather."

Harley's head swiveled in his direction. "No, of course not. It's g-great." She gestured toward the swing. "I mean, look at all the...wicker. And the straps. With the cotton cushion things. Those are really nice. Bet they wouldn't chafe at all."

Clay crossed the room, taking her hand and pulling her lightly against him. "It's okay. If you're not into the chair anymore, we can leave it here. I'm sure Jackson and Hannah would love to add it to their locked room downstairs."

Harley huffed softly. "You noticed that, too? I wonder if that's where they keep the whips and chains. "

"I don't know, but your sister seems pretty damned happy. Whatever they're doing, they must be doing it right." He cupped her jaw, rubbing his thumb gently over her skin. "I want to make you that happy. Tonight and every night."

"You do," Harley said, but she kept her gaze on his chest.

"Harley, look at me." He waited until her blue eyes lifted reluctantly to his. "Seriously, I don't give a shit about the swing. I thought it would be a fun surprise, but clearly it isn't. Don't waste another second thinking about it. "

"I can't help it," she said, the furrow between her brows deepening. "I'm not that person anymore, Clay. I can't be. You couldn't take me to a dungeon now. Not unless you wanted to impress the importance of birth control onto the young and impressionable people in the room."

Now it was his turn to frown. "You can't be serious."

"I can." She tried to pull away, but his arms tightened around her, holding her against him. "I am. If I sat in that swing right now, it would be the opposite of sexy. It would be a horror show of stretched out belly skin and saggy boobs and scrawny arms and legs because I haven't had the time or the energy to get to the gym and—"

"Stop it," Clay said. "I hate hearing you talk about yourself like that."

"Well, I'm sorry, but it's the truth," she said, throat working as she swallowed. "Under this dress, I'm like a rotted peach. Or a gremlin who recently had lap band surgery and hasn't had a chance to get the extra skin removed."

Clay laughed even as pain flashed through his chest. He didn't just hate hearing her talk this way; it was physically painful. Here she was, the most beautiful thing he'd ever seen, the most precious and irreplaceable, his best friend and the one person he couldn't live without. But when she looked at herself she saw a flappy-skinned gremlin.

Clearly he hadn't been doing a good enough job convincing her she was beautiful.

And that stopped. Right now.

"See?" A sad smile curved her lips. "It's funny because it's true. I'm basically golem. But with bigger boobs."

"You are not golem with bigger boobs," he said firmly. "But you are funny. I've laughed more the past year than the rest of my adult life combined."

She leaned into him with a sigh. "Good. It's nice to know I have something going for me now that my body is a lost cause."

"Your body is not a lost cause," he said, his hands smoothing down her back to mold to her amazing ass. "Your body is my fucking crack rock and I've been way too long without a fix. Now get your butt up on that bed and let me show you how much I love you."

Her breath rushed out. "Clay, I don't know if—"

"I said get your ass up on the bed," he said, delivering a firm swat to her bottom that made her cry out in surprise and heat flare in her eyes.

Trusting his gut, he lifted his hand, fisting it in her hair, holding her captive as he leaned down, letting his lips hover above hers as he spoke. "It's time to turn off your mind. Turn off your mind and let me turn on your body." His free hand drifted up, cupping her breast through her dress. "Let me fuck you until you come again and again, until you can't take any more pleasure and there is no doubt in your mind that you are the sexiest woman ever born."

"I might not be able to come," she whispered, even as her arms curled around his neck. "It might hurt too much. It hurt like hell the first time after I had Jasper."

"It's not going to hurt," he promised, backing toward the bed.

"I just don't want to disappoint you."

"You could never disappoint me. And I'm

going to get you so wet, so ready, that you're going to come the second I slide inside you." Her knees hit the back of the mattress and Clay reached up to flick the mosquito netting over their heads. "But first, I'm going to make you beg for it, sweetheart."

"Is that right?" she asked, lips curving as she arched a brow. "You know I don't beg easy, big guy."

"You don't do anything easy." He turned her around, reaching for the zipper on her dress. "That's part of your charm."

She shivered as he drew the zipper down, baring the elegant curve of her back. "Thank you," she whispered.

"For what?" He slid the straps down her arms, pressing a kiss to one lightly freckled shoulder. "I haven't even gotten started yet."

"For thinking my stubbornness is charming." She shivered again as he guided the dress over her hips and sent it falling to the floor, leaving her in nothing but a white strapless bra and white lace panties. "And for loving me even when it's hard."

Chest aching all over again, Clay wrapped

his arms around her, hugging her close, burying his face in her hair near the slope of her beautiful neck.

He wanted to tell her that he loved her more than anything in the world, more than life, more than even their children because there never would have been the miracle of Jasper or Will without the miracle of Harley first. He wanted to tell her that, after only a year of marriage, he felt so close to her that it was like a piece of her soul lived inside him, a piece that made him happier than he'd ever been before.

He wanted to tell her that loving her made him a better man, that the hard times made the sweet times even sweeter, and that there was nothing in the world he would rather do than be with her, skin to skin.

But some things are better said with actions than words. Some things can only be clearly communicated in the language of a kiss.

So he turned his beautiful, wounded, perfect, crazy, wild, sweet, wonderful wife around and he kissed her with everything in his heart.

CHAPTER SIX

Harley

*T*he first time it happened was last October. Clay had taken her and Jasper out for a fancy dinner to celebrate Jasper's first kindergarten report card. They'd had steak, grilled asparagus, and flourless chocolate cake, and Harley had stolen a couple of sips from Clay's glass of red wine, her OB having assured her a sip or two wouldn't hurt the baby.

They had laughed and rehashed the simple, beautifully ordinary events of their week, sharing silly family jokes and secret smiles, and at their table for three, love and gratitude had made the candles shine a little brighter.

Afterward, she and Clay had taken Jasper home and put him to bed before adjourning to their own bedroom where the rest of the world had disappeared.

There had been nothing but Clay's kiss, his hands, his love filling her up until she felt like her body would overflow and start leaking happiness all over the sheets. Gradually she had lost awareness of their separate bodies, their separate skins, as all the barriers between them were burned away.

She thought she'd made love before, but until that night, she hadn't come close. Before—even in the midst of the hottest, sweetest, most soul-altering sex she'd ever had—she'd always had one lid cracked. She had always been aware of the emergency exits, the primitive part of her brain busy mapping out an escape route, just in case one was needed.

But that night with Clay she'd run to him like the war was over, like the enemies were lying dead on the battlefield and all the evil in the world was smoldering in the ruins. She'd run to him, crashed into him, seeped through him, merging with the man she loved until there was no him or her, only them, *this*, a moment that lasted for eternity because it was the truth in a world full of lies.

And the truth was love and it was vaster than anything she had ever imagined.

Now, as Clay lengthened himself above her, kissing her until the kiss became a conversation and then a benediction—a promise that what they had transcended fragile bodies and any scars they bore—she remembered that this was who they were. They were two who had become one, and he was her irreplaceable beloved.

And she was the same to him.

Kissing him, feeling his warm hands sliding up her thighs, setting her heart to beating faster, she wondered how she could have doubted it, even for a moment.

"I've missed you so much," she murmured against his lips, breath catching as his fingers drew her panties to one side and his thumb found her clit.

"You, too. So much." His finger slid easily into where she was already wet. And there was no pain, only a wave of arousal that swept across her skin and the sense that she was exactly where she was supposed to be. "God, Harley. You feel so good. I can't wait to be inside you."

"Sounds like you might be the one who ends up begging," she teased, hands trailing down his lightly furred chest to find his nipples and pinching them with her fingers.

"Not a chance," he said with a groan. "Fuck. I never knew that could feel so good until you."

"Your other lovers were lacking in imagination," she said, breath rushing out as he continued to fuck her with his finger, stroking deeper, curling the digit until he was hitting that secret place inside her. "I would like to bite you right here." She pinched his right nipple, the flat brown disc that she knew tasted like salt and home and Clay. "But then I would have to move and you would have to stop doing that thing you're doing."

"Tough choice." Clay made a considering noise as he reached back to release the clasp on her bra with his free hand. "Why don't I bite you instead and we'll call it a win-win?"

Any retort she might have made tripped and fell into a ravine somewhere in her mind as he lowered his mouth and flicked his tongue across her nipple, then drew her inside his mouth and sucked hard enough to make her eyes roll back in her head. Immediately, every nerve ending in her body ignited and sharp, almost painful waves of pleasure coursed from her sensitive tip to burn between her legs. Her nipples hadn't quite recovered from her failed attempt to breastfeed Will. The skin was still raw and the nerves frayed. She had been avoiding touching herself there as much as possible—even in the shower.

But now, as Clay licked and sucked and bit, dragging his teeth lightly across her sensitized flesh, the pain bled into pleasure. Fresh heat rushed from between her legs to coat his finger and her blood pumped faster, until the heavy *thud thud thud* echoed in her ears, a drumbeat that underscored her increasingly urgent need.

She fisted her fingers in Clay's hair and lifted into his thrusts. "More. I want more of you."

"That doesn't sound like begging," he said, shifting his mouth to her left breast and circling her nipple with his tongue.

"Please," she said, spreading her legs wider in supplication. "Please give me more."

He added a second finger, stretching her until there was a flash of pain. But it was only a flash and soon it too was washed away by the desire flooding through her body, making her skin feel almost feverishly hot. He penetrated her with long, smooth strokes while the heel of his hand applied pressure to her clit, quickly driving her within kissing distance of the edge.

All she had to do was lean in and she would tumble over, but she didn't want to go without him.

"Now." Her hands slid down to claw her fingers into the thick muscles of his ass. "Please, I want you. I need you inside of me when I come."

"No, you're going to come for me first." His fingers rocked more insistently inside her. "On my hand, and then on my mouth. By the time I fuck you, you're going to be so wild I won't—"

Harley cried out, drowning out the rest of his words as her womb contracted and her pussy locked down on his fingers. Her orgasm was slow and disjointed, working through her in jerky fits and starts, like opening a door with hinges that hadn't been oiled for a long, long time.

But it was also fan-fucking-tastic.

She squeezed her eyes shut, seeing stars and white light exploding against a velvet sky and maybe God—at least a peek at the almighty infinite, if She was anywhere, She was where there was love like this—before she forced her eyes open with a gasp. She needed to look at Clay, to see his face while the pleasure he'd given her rocked her body from head to toe.

"Fuck." His features twisted as he bit down on his bottom lip. "You're so beautiful when you come. So fucking beautiful. I can't wait to make you go again."

Before she could respond, he was kissing his way down her body. He paused at her already kiss-swollen nipples to lick and tease, before moving farther down. He kissed her belly, making love to each inch of newly stretched out skin with a reverence that made her throat tight, before his tongue found the seam where her torso became thigh and began to trace his way even lower.

Her breath hitched and she shivered, her nipples tightening despite the warmth of the room.

"I've been dreaming about this for months." With his hands firm at the back of her knees, he spread her wide, groaning as he bared her pussy. "There you are. Look how wet you are, how wet and ready for me to take you with my mouth. I can't fucking wait to taste you."

"Clay, God, I—" Her words ended in a

sharp intake of breath as his tongue swept up her center, through the lips of her pussy to her clit, where he teased her in circles just long enough to make her squirm before transferring his attention to the rest of her swollen aching flesh.

His tongue probed and teased, exploring every inch of her, finding hidden places that were already sensitive from her first orgasm and pulsing his tongue against them until she writhed and moaned.

It felt like he was pushing on a bruise, painful, but exhilarating. With every rush of pleasure-pain, she came more savagely to life. It was like waking up from a dream, emerging from the cocoon of motherhood and new baby thrills and fears for the first time to realize that she was still a woman. She was still this man's woman, a fact he was making more increasingly clear with every flick of his talented tongue.

"You taste like the ocean." He thrust his stiff tongue deep into her channel—once, twice, three times—making her gasp and her hips lift off the bed, instinctively seeking more, deeper, harder.

"Like life," he continued, murmuring against her aroused flesh as his thumb circled her clit, drawing a whimper from low in her throat. "Like the beginning and the end and everything in between and I want it all with you. I want every fucking minute with you. Can you feel how much I need you?"

She sobbed his name, her breath coming so fast the ceiling started to spin. "Yes, I love you. I need you. So much. Please, I'm begging, Clay. I'm begging for you, I'll do anything. Just fuck me, you sadistic son of a bitch."

He made a sound, half groan half laugh, as he drove his tongue back inside her, plunging in and out as his thumb circled the top of her sex.

"Then come for me," he said, pulling away to lick her from top to bottom. "Come for me and then I'm going to be inside you so deep." His fingers plunged inside her while his tongue moved to her clit, flicking back and forth in a bone-melting rhythm. "I can't wait to feel you. My dick is fucking weeping for you right now."

"Please," Harley begged, her heels digging into the mattress and her thighs trembling. "Now, please, Clay. Oh God yes, I—"

She came so hard that something at the core of her detonated and her spirit swelled, expanding past the boundary of her skin to fill the room as Clay surged over her to cover her mouth with his. She opened for him, welcoming his tongue stroking through her mouth and the taste of him and her mingling in his kiss. She wrapped her arms and legs around him, welcoming everything he had to give, inviting him to take everything he needed.

And then his cock was at her opening, pushing inside, slow and steady, but unrelenting, gliding forward until every inch of him was buried inside of her and his balls pulsed in the seam of her ass. He stretched her walls, filling every inch of her. He was by far the thickest lover she'd ever had, but there was no pain, only pleasure, gratitude, and the sense that she was back where she belonged.

"So perfect." She sighed as the fear that it

would be too painful for her to make love to him properly this first time faded away.

"You're perfect," he whispered, holding still inside her, his breath puffing gently against her lips. "I'm sorry I failed you."

"Are you insane," she said, cupping his face in her hands. "Did you miss the two times you made me come like I was having an out of body experience? "

"But you didn't come when I pushed inside you the way I promised," he said, circling his hips, his pubic bone nudging her clit, making her breath catch. "I don't like to fail."

She wrapped her arms around his neck with a smile as she began to rock against him. "Then don't pull out until you get what you want. Then it still counts as the first thrust. Right, psycho?"

"I'm not a psycho." He reached down to cup her ass in his big hand, shifting the angle of their hips until his slightest movement caused new friction across the top of her sex. "I'm just invested in keeping my promises. Especially to you."

Harley looked up, meeting his gaze as he

continued to circle his hips, her heart stretching out its arms and falling into his eyes, knowing this man would always be there to catch her. "I know you are. Thank you."

"Stop thanking me," he whispered, eyes shining. "I should be thanking you. For our beautiful baby. And our amazing little man. And the fact that I get to wake up every day and feel…whole."

He swallowed, his throat working as the air between them filled with something far more powerful than simple lust. "I never imagined I could have a life like this. That I could be so in love that everything feels possible, just because you're here with me."

Harley blinked, sending tears slipping down her cheeks. "It's the same for me. Every single day."

"Then I don't want to hear you say another ugly word about yourself," he said, his rhythm between her legs becoming more urgent. "You never have and never will be anything but beautiful. Now come for me, let me watch you, let me see."

Harley held his gaze, fighting to keep her

eyes open as pleasure consumed her for the third time, washing over her and sucking her under, rolling her through the darkness. But she wasn't scared because Clay was there with her, calling her name as he began to move, drawing out her release until it was a thick rope binding them together. Until her third orgasm bled into her fourth and Clay came with her, his cock jerking deep inside her and his breath hot in her ear as he whispered words of love that her pleasure-drugged mind couldn't make sense of.

But she didn't need sense. She already had everything she needed, right there in her arms.

CHAPTER SEVEN

Clay

*T*hey lay twined together, the sweat cooling on their bodies, his fingers skimming up and down the soft skin of her back. They didn't talk, but they didn't need to. Everything had already been said.

Clay could feel the difference between them, a lightening in the air that made each breath come easier than the one before. They had found their way back to each other, the way they always had and always would.

And soon, their family would be safe and they would only worry about the things normal people worried about. Like how Will would ride out his first cold and whether or not Jasper would end up in the same class with his best friend for first grade.

"But I'm not sure we'll ever be completely normal," he murmured aloud.

Harley pressed a kiss to his chest. "What did I miss? I'm not as good at reading your mind as you are at reading mine."

He hugged her closer. "Just thinking about the future and how nice it will be to be living a simpler life."

"It's been pretty amazing so far," she said, fingers curling around his hip. "And I've got a feeling things are only going to get better from here on out."

"I like it when you have feelings like that," he said, hoping she was right.

Either way, he didn't regret the things he'd kept from her. Learning that someone had sent a hit man after her husband when she was six months pregnant, right as she was starting to feel safe again after the nightmare with Marlowe, would have made the end of her pregnancy as stressful as the beginning.

He hadn't wanted that for her or the baby. He and Jackson had both decided to keep the attempts on their lives from their wives, the better to give the sisters a shot at the normal life they'd both been denied for so long. Knowing Harley, if she'd learned about the attack, she wouldn't have stopped digging into the shooter's background until she found the same clues he'd found, the ones that had led him right to Stewart Mason's door.

He'd wanted to spare her that, too. She already knew that her father was a ruthless son of a bitch, but trying to kill the father of his daughter's children before the second one was even born was an ugly new low, even for Stewart.

Better for Senator Mason to be put away for one of his many other crimes—the sooner, the better.

Which meant Clay had a phone call to return ASAP.

"We should probably get cleaned up," he said, glancing at the clock on the bedside table. "Our reservation is in half an hour."

"Shit! I had no idea it was that late." Harley bolted into a seated position, snatching her underwear and bra from the end of the bed. "Give me ten minutes, then you can jump in the shower with me if you want."

"Nope." Clay stretched his arms overhead, admiring the view as she scooted off the bed and bent to retrieve her dress. "I'm going to stay sticky. I like knowing I have you all over me underneath my clothes."

"I know this about you," she said, shooting him a narrow look over her shoulder. "And I still can't decide if that's romantic or disgusting."

"Romantic," he assured her. "Now be quick, woman. I'm starving."

"Like a bunny," she said, pinching his toe on her way by, making him smile.

But the grin faded as she circled around the bed and out of his line of sight. It was time to make a call that might ruin the rest of their night, but it couldn't be helped. Austin, the man he had tailing Stewart, had been given strict orders not to make contact unless it was an emergency. Clay had already put him off for an hour—Austin had texted just as he and Harley were checking into the hotel.

Time to find out what Stewart fucking Mason was up to now.

Clay waited until he heard the bathroom door shut and the water turn on before pulling on his clothes and reaching for his phone. He hit the call button and stepped out onto the lanai, where the ocean breeze should keep his conversation from being heard if Harley was faster with her shower than usual.

"This better be good," he said when Austin picked up.

"It's not," Austin said, confirming his fears. "Stewart's gone, and so far I haven't had any luck tracking him down. It's like he vanished off the face of the earth."

Clay's brows drew tight together. "Gone? How is he gone? You were supposed to be following him."

"I did. I tailed him to his house three days ago. Once the car went into the garage, it never came back out again, and there's been no activity on the helicopter pad or any other vehicles coming into or out of the estate."

He frowned harder. "Then how do you know he's gone?"

"It's not like him to stay put for that long," Austin said. "Last night, I started to worry that I'd missed something so this morning I had Kent bring me the thermal imaging goggles. There are four people in the house, instead of the usual five, and all of them are too small to be Stewart. I don't know how he did it, but he ditched me."

Clay cursed softly before glancing back into the hotel room. Harley was out of the bathroom, letting her hair down from its clip and slipping into her dress.

He turned back to face the dark ocean. "Keep looking for him. And let me know as soon as you have any leads. I'll touch base with my associate, see if he has any information, and text you whatever I find out. I probably won't have time to call again tonight but contact me if there are any developments."

Clay ended the call and shot Jackson a quick text—

We've lost eyes on the mark. He's on the move, but we don't know where. Let me know if you have any leads for my guy and keep close tabs on everyone there.

Only a few seconds passed before Jackson texted back—

Will do. I'll reach out to my people and be in touch. Try to enjoy your night. Nothing is going to happen to Jasper or Will on my watch.

"What's up?" Harley asked, slipping her arms around his waist from behind.

She'd been so quiet, he hadn't heard her coming, a fact that disturbed him more than it usually would. Harley had a soft step and years of practice sneaking around, but he didn't like anyone taking him by surprise, not when Stewart was obviously up to something.

"Just checking in with Jackson," he said, sliding the phone back into his pocket. "Making sure the boys are doing okay. He said everything's fine."

Harley laughed as he turned in her arms.

"What?" he asked, unable to keep from returning her smile. He was worried, but she was beautiful and it felt like forever since he'd seen that particular grin on his wife's face. It was her wicked grin, the one that meant he was in for a night filled with the best kind of trouble.

"Nothing," she said, wrists linking behind his neck. "You're just cute. The big bad former spy who can't go more than an hour without checking up on his kids."

"It's been an hour and a half." Clay let his palms wander down to cup her bottom through her dress and gave a squeeze. "And I'm still big and bad. I think I just proved that, Mrs. Hart. But if you need a reminder, I can drag your fine ass back to bed right now."

She laughed low in her throat, an unabashedly sexy sound that made Clay's cock thicken in his pants. "Tempting, but if we don't get going, we'll miss our reservation. And someone I know said they were starving."

"I'm never so hungry I'll pass up a chance to fuck you." He leaned down to capture her mouth for a long, sweet kiss that was about to take a turn for the not-so-sweet when she pulled away and pressed a finger to his lips.

"Later," she said softly. "Let's go eat. I want to take you out and show you off without worrying about cutting up someone else's meat or making them eat their vegetables."

He smiled. "Jasper is great about eating his vegetables."

"Yes, he is. But you know what I mean."

"I do," he said, fingers twining through hers. "Let's go, build up our strength for round two, three, and four."

Harley laughed and a few moments later they were out the door, wandering hand in hand along the dimly lit path leading back to the heart of the resort.

Clay kept his posture loose and his gait easy, trying not to give away how eager he was to be somewhere less isolated. The privacy he'd been so grateful for an hour ago suddenly seemed like a liability, something that would make it easier for Stewart or his hired thugs to get in, do their worst, and get out again without being observed.

You're being crazy.

No one knows where you are, not even your parents, and you used a fake name when you booked the charter flight from Tahiti to Samoa.

If Stewart's sudden disappearance has something to do with you—and there's no reason to believe it does—he's going to need a lot more than three days to track you down.

The thought was rational, reasonable, and should have been comforting. But as he and Harley joined the line of people waiting beside the tiki-torch illuminated entrance to the resort's five-star restaurant, he couldn't shake the feeling that something wasn't right. He'd spied on enough people during his years in the CIA that he had a sixth sense when the shoe was on the other foot.

As he turned to press a kiss to his wife's forehead, he scanned the crowd behind her. There were people gathered at the poolside bar, an ever-thickening crowd spinning on the dance floor, and couples sipping drinks in heavily cushioned cabanas scattered throughout the darkness, shadowed by plantings designed to afford privacy. He didn't notice anyone who seemed to be paying

Harley and him obvious attention, but that didn't mean they weren't there.

The Malolo's midsummer luau was one of the biggest parties on the island and the resort was packed with visitors and locals enjoying a balmy tropical night out.

The crowd was so thick that a sniper could hide in plain sight, biding his time until he could pick Harley and Clay off like fish in a barrel.

Clay tried to banish the thought, but when the hostess showed them to a table in the center of the outdoor restaurant, he shook his head and motioned to another at the edge of the seating area. It was darker and offered no view of the lagoon, but it was most definitely out of the line of fire.

Better safe than sorry, and better paranoid than dead. Those were his mottos and he was sticking to them until he knew that Stewart Mason was locked behind bars.

CHAPTER EIGHT

Harley

What part of "big news" and "we need to meet" don't you understand?

Harley glanced down at her phone, forcing her expression to stay impassive as she let it drop back into her clutch.

Fucking Dominic.

He had a gift for contacting her at the

absolute worst times. If she didn't know better, she would think he knew when she was alone with Clay and was deliberately trying to expose the secrets they'd both been keeping for the past year.

Dom and Clay certainly weren't friends—Dom hated Clay with an intensity he didn't bother to hide, and Clay thought Dom was a creep who had taken advantage of Harley during a vulnerable time in her life—but the two men did occasionally brush elbows on the job. Six months ago, Dom had become a CIA informant, striking a deal to pave his way back to life on the right side of the law. He continued to haunt the fringes of the criminal underground while supplying Central Intelligence and the FBI with the information they needed to take down some of the big name bad guys he had worked for in the past.

Men like her father, though Dom had agreed to keep his mouth shut about Stewart until they had Mallory safely in hand.

They needed Stewart free in order to track his communications with the man who "owned" the girl. A year ago, Dom had been close to locating the half sister Harley had never met, but days before he was due to raid the compound where she was being held, Stewart had arranged for Mallory to be moved. Since then, her father had kept her captors on the move and Dom struggling to play catch up.

But maybe now he had caught up. Maybe that was the big news.

Harley picked up her glass of white wine, taking a long sip of the cool liquid, curiosity getting the better of her. She had to get Dom to spill the beans over the phone, no matter how paranoid he was about his calls being tapped.

Her phone buzzed again. Keeping her expression relaxed, she slipped her hand into her purse and tipped the screen up.

So put down your wine, excuse yourself from the table, and meet me behind the bathrooms by the kiddie pool. This won't keep.

Her heart dropped into her stomach.

Holy shit. He was here, somewhere out there in the darkness.

Watching her.

She set her wine down a little too hard.

"Who's that?" Clay asked, still scanning the menu he held. Thank God. If he'd been looking at her face when she read that last message, he would have known instantly that something was up. She wasn't nearly as good at hiding her emotions as she used to be.

She was going soft, a fact that didn't bother her most of the time, but right now it sure as hell did. The old Harley would have had her guard up and her feelers out. She would have been scanning the crowd for potential predators instead of dwelling on how handsome her husband looked with the candlelight playing across the planes of his face.

"Hannah," she lied. Explanations would have to wait until after she put out this fire. She had to get to Dom before he did something crazy. If he'd followed her to Samoa, he was clearly off the rails.

"She said it wasn't urgent and not to worry," Harley continued, pulling her napkin from her lap and placing it beside her bread plate. "But I should step out and call her anyway. She wouldn't have texted twice unless she was worried about something."

"Do you want me to come with you?" he asked, setting his menu down.

"No! Don't be silly. Hold our table." She scooted her chair back. "And if our waiter comes back, order the fish for me. I don't care what the fresh catch is, I'm sure it will be amazing."

Clay frowned as she stood. "Are you sure? Maybe we should hold off on ordering until we know we're not needed at the house."

Harley waved a hand through the air. "I'm sure we're fine to stay. Hannah would have called if it were a real emergency." She forced a smile, hoping it was too dark for Clay to see the pulse hammering at her throat. "Order another glass of wine for me, too, will you?" She winked. "I plan on getting a little drunk and letting my husband take advantage of me."

Clay's eyes flashed. "That sounds like an excellent plan. But be careful, okay? Don't step into any dark corners. Parties like this can get dangerous after the liquor's been flowing."

"I will." She leaned across the table to press an impulsive kiss to his cheek, silently promising that she would tell him everything she'd been keeping from him the second she was sure Mallory was safe.

Right after she gave Dom free rein to deliver her father's criminal history to the CIA wrapped up in a nice little bow.

"Be right back," she whispered before turning and weaving her way across the patio. The restaurant's awnings were rolled up tonight in a nod to the lovely weather and every table in the place was filled with people laughing, drinking, and canoodling under the stars.

As Harley passed the other tables, she let her gaze slide from one face to another, certain none of these happy, sunburned, half-wasted people had ever worked for a drug lord, had their father threaten to do terrible things to their son, or spent a year fighting to save their half sister from human traffickers. These were ordinary people, who took their safety and right to pursue happiness for granted. They didn't go to bed worried for the lives of their family.

But then, they probably didn't wake up feeling breathlessly grateful for another day, either. For all the misery her father and Marlowe and all the other dark forces from her past had caused her, they had also made her grateful for the miracle of an ordinary life.

She treasured every moment she spent walking Jasper to school and helping with homework, loved spending Sunday afternoons at her in-laws' farm playing baseball in the backyard, and lived for lazy mornings making pancakes while Clay, Jasper, and baby Will snuggled on the couch watching cartoons. Since her return from the dead, prices of her old artwork had tripled and her new pieces were sold before she could even finish them, but it wasn't money or fame that made her smile when she woke up every morning.

It was those precious, everyday moments that were locked away in her heart, filling her with joy, hope, and the determination to keep fighting to eradicate the shadows from her life one by one.

Which made her wonder what the hell she

was going to do about Dom.

She needed him to do the legwork she couldn't, but him showing up here unannounced was a clear violation of their working arrangement. They'd only met a few times in the past year and had always planned their meetings at least a week in advance.

Not to mention the fact that no one, not even Clay's parents, had known where they were headed this summer. They had deliberately kept their travel plans secret, which inspired a host of other unsettling questions.

Had Dom been tracking her movements? Had he installed that spyware he was so leery of on her cell phone so he would know where she was at all times? And if he had—why?

A few minutes ago, Harley would have sworn that any romantic feelings or regrets were in the past for her and Dom. She knew he'd been hurt when she'd called things off, but she had never pretended that she felt anything more than friendship and physical attraction for him. And she suspected his broken heart had more to do with losing a stand-in for Hannah than any deep and abiding feelings for her.

Dom had always had a thing for her sister, but Harley understood. Most people with any sense would choose sweet and sunny over sarcastic and complicated—and those were some of Harley's better traits.

But maybe she'd been wrong about Dom letting go and moving on…

The thought made her pause at the edge of the kiddie pool, where a map of the resort was illuminated by flickering tiki torches on either side. She didn't need to look at the map—she could see the restrooms where she was supposed to meet Dom from where she stood—but she couldn't ignore the unease prickling across her skin, raising the hairs on the back of her neck. No matter how much she trusted Dom, she wasn't sure she wanted to be alone with him right now.

At least not until she knew what this was really about.

Trusting her gut, she slipped her phone from her clutch and pulled up his contact information. The kiddie pool was deserted this time of night—the plastic pirate ship's water cannons were turned off and the slides shut down—so there was no one around to overhear her conversation.

He answered on the second ring. "So I guess you got the email."

Harley blinked. "No, I didn't. I've been traveling with Clay and the kids all day. I haven't had a chance to check my private messages."

"Fine, well, to sum it up, we're screwed. Again. I got to the compound in Georgia a day too late. It might have only been a few hours. There were still dirty dishes in the sink with food on them that hadn't had time to get crusty yet." Dom let out a ragged sigh. "I threw a few of them across the room before I left."

"I'm sorry, I know it's frustrating." Harley leaned back against the map, keeping an eye on the path, lowering her voice as a couple who'd clearly had a few too many mai tais wove their way through the darkness toward her. "But we can't give up, Dom."

"Oh, I'm not giving up," he said. "I'm just

getting pissed. What the fuck is wrong with your father? Why is making an innocent girl suffer so fucking important to him that he'll exert this much time, energy, and money to keep her his prisoner?"

"Because that's the way Stewart Mason operates. It's all about winning and losing with him. Mallory isn't a person; she's a chess piece. I guarantee my father hasn't spent a single second thinking about her feelings or her pain or the human consequences of his actions. It's the same way with Hannah and me. He just wants different things from us."

"You're queens and Mallory is a pawn," Dom said bitterly.

Harley ran a hand through her hair. "Yeah. I guess. Something like that. I don't know. But he's going to lose eventually. As long as we don't give up."

"You think?"

"I know," Harley said, hating to hear him sounding so defeated. Maybe that's why he'd come to meet her here. Maybe he was desperately in need of a face-to-face pep talk. It was still a little weird, but if anyone could understand how demoralizing her father could be, it was Harley. "He's pushing seventy. If nothing else, he'll be dead soon."

Dom grunted. "No, he won't. The monsters always live forever. It's the good people who love their kids and take in foster children who get stage four colon cancer and die before their time."

Harley frowned. "That's a pretty specific example."

"Yeah, well." Dom sniffed. "I lost a friend last week. Cancer fucking sucks."

"It does. I'm so sorry, Dom." Harley spun on her heel, starting across the quiet pool deck near the abandoned kiddie pool. "I'm coming to give you a hug right now. It sounds like you need one."

"Thanks, but that's probably a little impractical."

"Why?" Harley asked. "A hug is a hug. Friends hug all the time."

"I'm still in Georgia," he said. "Aren't you somewhere halfway across the world by now? I'm assuming the Hart family doesn't summer somewhere normal like Florida or Myrtle

Beach."

Harley's footsteps faltered. "What about the bathrooms by the kiddie pool? The text you sent said to you meet you there."

"I didn't send you a text, Harley," he said, his words sending a shiver of apprehension dancing up her spine. "Get out of there. Wherever you are. Get out, get to a crowded place, and call Clay."

"I am," Harley whispered as she reversed direction, hustling back across the pool, keenly aware that there could be someone behind the bathrooms listening to her every word. "I'll call you in five minutes. If I don't—"

Her words became a gasp as a man stepped out of the bushes to her left, blocking her way. She recognized his face immediately.

It was Eli, Cutter's thug, one of the men who had intended to drag her into Marlowe's maze last Midsummer Eve and take turns with her before he killed her for Marlowe's amusement. Marlowe was dead, Cutter was, too, but Eli was alive and well, and if the hypodermic needle in his hand was any clue, clearly ready to finish what he'd started this time last year.

Harley turned to run, planning to cut through the foliage on the other side of the pool and make a break for the lobby, but Eli was too fast. She barely had time to register the sound of heavy footsteps on the concrete behind her before she felt the jab of the needle shoving into the place where her shoulder met her neck.

She cried out, her phone falling from her hand as her knees buckled. The world went black before her body hit the ground.

CHAPTER NINE

Clay

*I*t would normally have taken fifteen minutes for Clay to get worried about Harley, but tonight wasn't a normal night.

Tonight was a night with Stewart Mason missing in action. The longer Clay had to mull over the problem of the AWOL Senator, the more certain he became that Stewart's vanishing act was no coincidence.

Jackson's people were days, maybe hours, away from having everything they would need for Clay to get a warrant for Stewart's arrest. A man didn't become as powerful as Mason without having big ears in important places. There was a significant chance that someone had tipped Stewart off that it was time for him to run.

And if that were true, Stewart wouldn't just be furious, he would be dangerous. A cornered monster is bad enough. A cornered monster on the verge of losing everything could be deadly.

Janis Joplin sang, "Freedom's just another word for nothing left to lose."

But what about when your freedom was threatened, too? That was when you truly had nothing. No more time, no more leverage, no way out except with your finger wrapped around the trigger of a gun.

Some people would choose to put that gun to their own head, but Clay wasn't naïve enough to think that Stewart Mason would spare his family by choosing suicide. No, he would want to cause a little more suffering on his way out, and his estranged daughter was near the top of a short list of people Stewart loved to torment the most.

Clay pushed his chair back, preparing to go look for Harley and stay glued to her side until she finished her phone call.

But before he could stand, an older man in a blue-and-white flowered Aloha shirt, holding a swaddled baby, slipped by the hostess with a smile and a nod in Clay's direction and started across the crowded restaurant toward him.

Clay's mouth went dry and his brain squirmed in his skull, rejecting the information being telegraphed from his eyes. Monsters didn't appear out of thin air simply because you were thinking too hard about them.

This couldn't be happening. That couldn't be Stewart Mason walking toward him holding a baby.

Oh God. A baby. *Will.*

Clay vaulted from his seat, ready to snatch Will out of Stewart's arms and ask questions about how the hell the man had gotten his hands on his son later. But as Stewart stopped across the table, Clay noticed two very important things—

One: the baby wasn't Will. The infant had chubbier cheeks, darker eyebrows, and bow-shaped lips that made Clay think she was probably a girl, not a boy.

Two: Stewart had a gun in his left hand, pressed lightly to the baby's chest. It was mostly concealed beneath the white blanket wrapped around the child. But as Stewart faced Clay down across the table, he allowed the barrel of the gun to emerge into the night air.

"Good evening, Agent Hart," Stewart said, his blue eyes dancing with something a shade too manic to be victory. "I trust you're enjoying your stay at the Malolo."

"Put the baby down," Clay said softly, scanning the crowd behind Stewart, willing someone to look up and notice what was going on in this dark corner of the restaurant. But the other patrons were too busy enjoying themselves to sense that a predator had slunk into the center of the herd.

"You're not giving the orders, agent." The wrinkles on Stewart's lightly creased face deepened as he smiled. "This is what we're going to do. You're going to lead the way out of the restaurant, down the path past the pools, and through the gardens toward the lighthouse."

"I'll go with you, but you need to leave the baby here," Clay said. "I'll set her down by my chair. She's asleep, so she won't start crying right away. We'll have plenty of time to get out of the restaurant before—"

"You will walk at a leisurely pace," Stewart continued as if Clay hadn't spoken. "You will smile at anyone we might pass by, but you will not stop to chat. Most importantly, you will give no impression that anything is wrong. If you fail to obey my orders at any time between now and the moment our business is concluded, I will put my gun under this beautiful little girl's chin and pull the trigger."

The words connected like a fist to the gut.

Clay didn't know if it was the utter lack of human emotion in Stewart's voice or the fact that Clay had a baby exactly the same age as the one in Stewart's arms at home, but it was all he could do not to bend over and lose the bread he'd eaten all over the patio.

"Start moving," Stewart added pleasantly. "Or I will end the child's life right now. Thanks to you, Agent Hart, I no longer have any reason to pretend to be anything but what I am."

"A monster?" Clay moved around the table, swallowing hard against the bile rising in his throat.

"A realist," Stewart corrected, falling in behind Clay as he started for the exit. "And a pragmatist. Results are all that have ever mattered to me. Methodology should only come into question if the methods used have failed to deliver the desired results."

Clay nodded to the hostess as he passed by but didn't stop to explain where he was going. He had dealt with enough hostage situations to know when someone was bluffing. Stewart wasn't. If Clay stopped to speak to anyone between here and the lighthouse, Stewart would put a bullet through an innocent child.

And if he didn't try to signal for help or fight back, Stewart was going to kill him. If Clay let his mind flip and tumble, he could come up with other logical reasons for Stewart to have come all the way to Samoa to threaten him at gunpoint, but in his gut, he knew this wasn't about Stewart wanting to cut a deal or avoid extradition to the U.S.

This was Stewart finishing what he'd failed to do last January.

"If your desired results are reconciliation with Harley, this sure as hell isn't the way to do it." Clay slipped his hands into his pockets, keeping his gait relaxed even as he scanned the clusters of people around him for his wife. If she saw him walking anywhere with Stewart, she would know to go for help.

But so far there was no sign of her. She wasn't near the entrance to the restaurant or the path leading to the adult pool, where several other people were taking advantage of the relative silence to place a call.

"My daughter is a more complicated creature than you give her credit for," Stewart said. "Did she ever tell you about our hunting trips when she was small? She wasn't much of a shot, of course, at that age, but she loved it when it came time to skin the animals. Loved to get up to her elbows in the blood and gore and see what was hiding beneath the surface."

"No, she didn't mention that," Clay said. "But she has mentioned the times you made her stand in a corner until she wet her pants in order to humiliate her for crying when you thought she shouldn't. What was she, five years old when you started that shit?"

Stewart laughed softly. "She needed that kind of discipline. She's my child, that one. Always has been, from the moment she was born. And once I explain to her that you've ruined our family name and destroyed the empire I built for her and her sister, she'll see that you're an acceptable loss."

"You're wrong," Clay said though he knew there was no point trying to use logic with someone who found it acceptable to threaten an infant's life. "She loves our family. And me. When she learns what you've done, it will tear her apart. She will never be the same, and she won't let you anywhere near her or the kids again."

"She won't have a choice," Stewart said, a smug note in his voice Clay didn't understand until he added, "I've got enough evidence to prove she framed Jackson Hawke and tampered with evidence in a felony case, which carries a sizeable prison sentence on its own without lying under oath and all the rest of it."

"Bullshit," Clay said, fighting to keep his volume low. "I destroyed anything that could lead to a conviction in that case."

"You can't destroy what you don't know is there, agent. I've had everything I needed to prove my daughter was lying about her rape since the summer you both went over the guardrail in that car. I knew there would come a time when I would need leverage to keep my wild child in line."

Clay bit down hard on his bottom lip, silently cursing the sick bastard.

"If she doesn't agree to my demands," Stewart continued, "she won't see her children until they're too old to care about the woman who used to be their mother. She will spend the next fifteen to twenty years behind bars and the children will go to your parents."

Stewart fell silent as they passed two men talking too loudly about a woman in a white bikini they both apparently considered "theirs" for the night. Even if the men hadn't been wasted, they were too caught up in their own pointless drama to pay attention to anyone else's, and Harley was still nowhere in sight.

"They seem like such trusting people," Stewart added as Clay took the turn toward the lighthouse, moving through the gardens where there were even fewer people to observe his abduction. "They'll be unprepared for a visitor in the dead of night, come to pull Jasper and Will from their beds."

"You're never going to touch my kids. You're going to jail." Clay's hands balled into fists at his sides. "There's already a warrant out for your arrest."

"Not yet, but there will be soon enough," Stewart said. "Why do you think I'm here? On the lovely island of Samoa, where there is no extradition treaty in place with the United

States. That's why Ian Hawke's son chose the location, isn't it? Because of his troubles with the law?"

"The extradition treaty won't mean shit if you commit murder on the island." Clay searched the darkness on either side of the trail for anything he could use as a weapon. But the grounds were meticulously maintained. "They have their own justice system here and they prosecute killers the same way we do in the U.S."

"Then I guess I'll have to hope I'm clever enough not to get caught," Stewart said, before adding in a softer voice. "I meant what I said, agent. If you don't keep walking straight toward that lighthouse, where you will kneel down and take a bullet to your head like a man, I will kill this child. This baby whose only crime was having a mother who fell asleep in the hammock outside her hotel room, leaving the door open for me to duck inside."

Clay swallowed hard, his thoughts racing. But for the first time in a long time, he couldn't see any way out. He couldn't be responsible for the death of an infant. He couldn't choose his own life over that baby's, no matter how loudly a voice in his head insisted that he couldn't give up without a fight.

But sometimes fighting isn't an option.

Sometimes there is nothing left to do but make what peace you can in the time you have left.

A moment later, the lighthouse came into view in the bright blue moonlight, a lonely relic of another age, slowly decomposing on a cliff above the ocean. A cliff where the waves smashed against the jagged shore beneath, creating enough noise to cover the sound of a gunshot and ensure a body left there might not be found for weeks, long after Stewart Mason and his gun were gone.

CHAPTER TEN

Hannah

$\mathcal{I}$t was the perfect ending to a perfect night.

Hannah was snuggled on the cushy outdoor couch watching the last fifteen minutes of her favorite cartoon of all time projected on the stucco wall of her home, her beautiful, brilliant nephew was asleep on what was left of her lap, and the girls had finally stopped cartwheeling around in her belly and settled in for a nap of their own. Her entire pregnancy had passed in a warm, foggy haze of well-being and tonight she had more reason than ever to be feeling blessed and grateful.

So when the bottom dropped out of her stomach at a few minutes after ten o'clock and anxiety began to dance across her skin on little razor feet, it hit her hard. She reached for her phone and shot a quick text to Jackson upstairs, not wanting to shout and risk waking one or both of the kids.

Is Will okay?

After only a few seconds, Jackson replied, *Yes. Still sleeping, but I got the bottle out of the fridge to warm up for the ten p.m. feeding. I'll be ready when the time comes.*

Everything okay out there?

I checked on you a few minutes ago. Looks like Jasper's down for the count. Want me to come carry him up to bed or are you enjoying snuggle time?

Despite the dread spreading through her chest, Hannah smiled. She was used to Jackson checking up on her. It was part of his natural rhythm to be protective and a little paranoid, but the warming bottles and carrying little boys up to bed Jackson was new. She had never worried that her husband would be an amazing father—he had the biggest heart she'd ever known—but it was still wonderful to see him slipping so naturally into the role of daddy figure. Seeing him hold Will earlier this evening had been enough to bring tears to her eyes.

Happy tears, of course, because she was a happy pregnant woman, one of those annoyingly cheerful gestaters her sister had assured her drove the pregnant women who felt like their bodies had been possessed by foul-tempered aliens absolutely crazy.

But despite the sweet text and her sweeter thoughts about her husband, the nervous feeling pricking at her skin only got worse. *Yes, come down, would you? Something feels wrong.*

"What's up, sunshine?" Jackson's concerned voice came from the deck above her. "You and the girls all right?"

She tilted her head back and smiled to reassure him before she whispered, "We're all fine. It's nothing like that. Just need to talk."

"I'll grab the monitor from my office and be right down."

As Jackson's silhouette faded back into the shadows, Hannah punched out another quick text. This time to Harley. *Text or call as soon as you can, okay? Nothing's wrong, the boys are fine, I'm just having a worry wart moment. Want to make sure you're okay and having a good time.*

Her thumb hovered over the send button, debating whether she should interrupt her sister's first date night in a year to soothe her own frayed nerves, but then she pressed the green dot and sent the message swooping out into the world. She loved Harley and she was happy for her and wanted to do nice things for the sister she'd reconnected with last August. But Harley had also been a long-standing pain in her ass. She owed Hannah a few "get out of worry" free passes.

And once Hannah explained that her anxiety was growing more focused on Harley with every passing minute, her sister would understand why she felt compelled to reach out.

When they were younger, their twin telepathy had been eerily strong. They'd always seemed to know when the other was in trouble, whether it was Harley having a knockdown, drag out fight with her man of the moment, or Hannah having a nervous breakdown in science class because she'd studied the wrong chapter and was in the middle of failing a test.

On that particular day, Harley had been so concerned that she'd gotten a hall pass and walked by Hannah's classroom. She'd paused at the door, catching Hannah's gaze and rolling her eyes when she realized what was giving her twin an anxiety-fueled heart attack.

Harley clearly hadn't thought failing a test was worth all the angst, but she'd still pulled the fire alarm on her way to the bathroom. The entire school had filed outside. By the time they were allowed back into the classroom, it was time for the final bell to ring. Hannah's science teacher had gathered up the test papers and announced they would finish the test the next day, giving Hannah a night to study the correct chapter.

She smiled at the memory. In the not too distant past, when she was still busy unpacking all the pain and regret her sister had brought into her life, it had been easy to forget the times when Harley had been her hero.

"What's on your mind, beautiful?" Jackson's hands landed gently on her shoulders, his thumbs pressing into the knots on either side of her spine. "You're tense."

She glanced down to make sure Jasper was still asleep. "I'm worried about Harley. I just sent her a text, but she hasn't replied."

Jackson circled around the couch, setting the baby monitor on the snack-laden table before settling beside her. "Maybe she and Clay are...indisposed."

Hannah wrinkled her nose at him. "That's a stuffy way to put it."

"I'm stuffy, what can I say?" he said, wrapping an arm around her as she leaned against his chest. "You don't think they noticed the locked room downstairs, do you?"

Hannah snorted softly. "You better believe they did. Nothing gets past Harley, and Clay used to be a spy. I'm sure they noticed, hypothesized, and drew conclusions. Probably accurate conclusions, knowing my sister."

"Good," Jackson said. "Then they'll have some idea what we're giving up in order to host them for a month."

"Oh hush." Hannah nudged him in the side. "You know we aren't giving up much. I'm too big to have any real fun."

Jackson kissed the top of her head. "You're always real fun."

Hannah nibbled her bottom lip. "What will we tell the kids if they ask about the mysterious locked door?"

"Well, Will is too little to be asking much and Jasper is a good kid. We'll just tell him that's a room where we keep grown-up things that aren't appropriate for children."

Hannah pulled away from his chest, glancing up at him in the glow of the projector screen. "No, I mean *our* kids. What do we tell them? I know it won't be a big deal at first, but eventually, there will come a time when they'll realize that not everyone's parents have a locked room where they aren't allowed to go."

Jackson stood, pulling one of the footstools over and sitting down facing her before drawing her feet into his lap. "Our kids will feel loved and safe," he said, his thumbs circling her swollen ankles, drawing a soft sigh from her lips. "And kids who feel loved and safe don't ask as many questions. And even kids who grow up the way we did assume their lives are normal. When was the first time you realized that not everyone had a nanny, lived in a mansion, or had a psychopath for a father?"

"Point taken." She rested a gentle hand on Jasper's head, loving the silky soft feel of his hair, and loving that her sister had raised such a completely normal, happy little boy even more.

If Harley could do it, surely Hannah could, too, no matter how poor her parenting role models had been.

"But if it becomes an issue, we can rent a space somewhere nearby," Jackson continued, his touch sending waves of pleasure coursing through her, a sharp contrast to the worry still making her tongue tap behind her teeth. "We'll hire someone we trust to watch the girls and you and I will go have our time somewhere else. It will be the best of both worlds."

She hummed noncommittally as she flipped her phone over on the cushion.

Still no text from Harley.

Jackson squeezed her ankle. "It will be. I won't settle for anything less. And if you need convincing of that, I'll rent a space while your sister and Clay are here and show you exactly how serious I am about making sure you get what you need from me. Everything you need. No matter what else is going on with our lives or how things change."

Hannah shivered as the memory of last night danced through her mind. She'd needed pillows to make kneeling at Jackson's feet comfortable, but that hadn't stopped her. Or him. His touch had been gentle, respectful of the new limitations of her body, but his dominance of her had been as complete as always. He had claimed her, body and soul, leaving her a trembling, whimpering wreck on the floor of their playroom.

And then he'd carried her up to their bedroom and drawn her a bath, sliding the soap over her body until her soul and skin made peace with each other. Afterward, they'd made love again, this time in their bedroom, the place where they were just Jackson and Hannah, not master and submissive. Jackson had spooned her on the bed, lifting her leg over his thigh and sliding his cock inside her from behind, inch by careful inch, until she was filled with the man she loved, surrounded by his scent, his warmth, and the safety of his body shielding her from the world.

She shivered. "No, sir. I don't need a reminder, but thank you."

"My pleasure," Jackson murmured. "Always my pleasure, sunshine."

"But I would like to call the resort," she said, tapping the screen on her phone with one finger. "I've got a bad feeling that something's wrong with Harley. My twin sense is tingling."

Jackson arched a brow. "Your twin sense?"

"I haven't felt it in years, but we haven't been in the same time zone for years, either. Back when we were kids, I always knew when Harley was in trouble. I would get this ugly, black feeling in my chest." Hannah picked up the phone, silently willing her sister to respond. "And I've got it bad right now."

"Call her," Jackson said, surprising her.

"But I can't, can I," Hannah said even as she swiped the arrow to the right, preparing to make the call. "That would be even more disruptive than texting."

"You're afraid for her. Call her and let her know your twin sense is tingling. She'll understand." He shrugged. "Or she won't and you'll know she hasn't changed as much as Clay seems to think she has."

Hannah frowned, bringing her hand to cover Jasper's ear. "Stop," she whispered. "Not in front of Jasper. Even if he's asleep. Be good."

"Good isn't my strong suit," Jackson said, his hand sliding up her calf, sending a different breed of tingles dancing across her skin.

"Behave," she said, smiling as she hit the call button. But the smile didn't last long. By the time the phone had rung six times with no answer and the line clicked over to voicemail, her worry had reached a new high.

Her voice shook as she left her message. "Harley, call me. I'm worried. I'm afraid something bad has happened. It's a twin tingle moment if you know what I mean. So call me and promise me you're okay or I'm going to worry all night." She sighed before signing off with a soft, "Never ever."

It was what they had said to each other since they were small, something deeper than "I love you." She hadn't felt compelled to say it for a long time, but now, sitting here feeling helpless to protect her twin from whatever bad thing was happening to her, the words meant something.

For years, she'd believed her sister was dead. She never ever wanted to wake up to another morning like that again.

"I'll call Clay," Jackson said, pulling his phone from his back pocket. "He contacted me earlier. Maybe he has his phone with him, and they left Harley's in the room."

"Thanks, babe." Hannah wiggled her toes nervously in his lap while his call connected and the phone rang and rang.

"Voicemail," Jackson said with a frown before leaving his message. "Clay. Call me. It's urgent."

"Don't say that!" Hannah said as he hung up. "He might think there's something wrong with the kids."

"Good. Then he'll call back faster." Jackson stood and leaned over to scoop Jasper into his arms. "I'll tuck this one in. You want to go feed Will his bottle?"

"Yes, oh man, I didn't ever hear him." She leveraged herself to her feet, grabbing the monitor, which was emitting snuffly, grunty, baby sounds, the fussy precursor to a full-fledged hunger wail. "Help him brush his teeth, Jackson," she called after her husband. "He shouldn't go to bed with all that sugar on his teeth."

"On it," Jackson said, evidently meaning more than brushing Jasper's teeth.

By the time Hannah finished feeding and

burping Will, changed his diaper, and rocked him back to sleep, Jackson was standing in the living room with one of his friends from work. One of his very big, very scary-looking friends, who divided their time between bulking up at the gym and serving as bodyguards for visiting dignitaries. But she knew from experience that Neville was a gentle giant. The only thing truly scary about the six foot five Polynesian was how good he was at cards. He took her for her entire jar of pennies every time the security firm boys came over for poker night.

"Hello, Neville. Good to see you," Hannah said, running a hand through her wild hair as she shifted her gaze to Jackson. "What's going on?"

"Neville is going to stay here with you and the kids while I go check on Harley and Clay."

"Oh no, you don't have to do that," Hannah said, even as relief and gratitude spread through her chest. "I'm sure they're fine. We can just keep trying to call."

"You're not sure they're fine," Jackson said. "And neither am I. Clay and I have been working on something behind the scenes and it's been coming to a head the past few days. There's a chance it could have put him and Harley in danger."

"Working on something." Hannah propped her hands on her hips. "What kind of something, Jackson?"

Jackson exchanged a loaded look with Neville, before crossing the room and drawing her into the kitchen. "The kind of something I don't have time to tell you about right now," he said once they were alone.

"You've had plenty of time before," she insisted, folding her arms across her chest. "Why is this the first I'm hearing of this secret project? Which I'm sure is dangerous and probably illegal?"

"It's not illegal," Jackson said, meeting her challenging gaze with an unflappable one. "And it's the first you're hearing of it because keeping you safe is my number one priority. And that includes keeping your blood pressure down and your worry level low while you're carrying our children."

"That's a bunch of crap, Jackson," she said,

fighting to keep her voice down. "I'm pregnant, I'm not a child."

"No, you're not, but you've been fighting high blood pressure this entire pregnancy. The last thing you needed was more stress, especially pointless stress. There is nothing you could have done to improve the situation Clay and I are dealing with. Therefore, there was no point in you being informed."

"This isn't the playroom." She frowned harder, hating the helpless, out-of-the-loop feeling throwing her off balance. "You don't get carte blanche to decide what's best for me."

"Yes, I do," Jackson said in an infuriatingly calm voice. "You can be angry with me if you need to be, but I would do the exact same thing again. If the stress of knowing the truth had caused you to lose the girls, I never would have forgiven myself. And if something had happened to you in the process, I would have had nothing left to live for. You are my world. Nothing else matters."

Hannah swallowed, torn between being touched and the anger and frustration still pumping through her blood.

"I had no other choice, sunshine," Jackson continued in a softer voice. "I hope you can understand that eventually. Now I have to go. Stay inside with Neville and stay away from the windows."

"Oh God, Jackson, what's going on?" Hannah tangled her fingers in his shirt, holding tight. "Why do we need to stay away from the windows?"

"Because I love you," he said, leaning down to press a kiss to her forehead. "And I would rather be paranoid and secretive and overly careful than risk one hair on your head." And then his lips moved to hers, claiming her mouth with a deep, tender, heartfelt kiss that assured her every word he'd said was true.

She was loved—deeply, fiercely. And if it wasn't always as conventional as she might like, that was okay. She'd known from the start that Jackson would never be entirely domesticated. He was wild and so was their love, and despite moments like this, she wouldn't have it any other way.

"Be careful," she whispered against his lips

as he pulled away. "Be so very careful and come back safe."

"I'll call you as soon as I have any news."

They moved back into the living room and, after a few more words with Neville, Jackson hurried out of the house. Hannah listened to the SUV driving away down the gravel road and sighed before turning to Neville with a tight smile.

"Poker or blackjack?" she asked. "What's your poison? Because there's no way I'm going to be able to sleep until whatever is going on is over."

Neville smiled, a warm grin that lit up his usually stoic face. "You know I'm a poker, man. And don't worry, everything will be fine. Except your pennies. Those will soon be mine."

Hannah nodded. "Of course they will. I expect nothing less."

As she and Neville got out the cards and set up at the kitchen table, she tried to think of nothing but the children sleeping safely in their beds and how nice it was to share an evening with a friend.

But in her mind, she kept drifting to another place, a dark, damp, musty-smelling place where she feared something terrible was happening to the woman who would always be one of the biggest parts of her heart.

CHAPTER ELEVEN

Harley

*H*arley's body had always been every bit as voracious as her mind.

Her metabolism ran high and when she was younger and less concerned with nutrition, she would get so swept up in whatever drama was in the works that she would forget to eat and end up walking skin and bones. Without adequate calorie intake, her body quickly turned to consuming itself, its hunger so insatiable it had no care for the fact that it had already devoured all the fat on her frame and was now busily digesting muscle tissue she needed in order to survive.

It was the same with drugs and alcohol.

From her first glass of wine or puff of marijuana, her body had immediately adjusted, needing more and more to achieve the same effect. It was why she rarely drank. The amount of wine she needed to consume to feel even a slight buzz was unwisely large.

But her swift metabolism and propensity to adjust to foreign substances quickly were also why she began to wake sooner than her captor expected.

Before they had learned to trust each other again, Clay had injected her with a sedative twice, and clearly, her body remembered what to do with those particular chemicals. It burned away the last of the haze in time for Harley to see the man who'd taken her making up a rusted twin bed in the corner of a dimly lit room.

A quick scan of her body revealed that she

was slumped in a chair—a wheelchair maybe, since there were footrests beneath her feet and the soft give of leather beneath her sit bones—but that her hands and legs were unbound. Eli hadn't tied her up. Maybe he intended to tie her to the bed he was preparing? Or maybe he didn't anticipate needing to bind her since he was bigger and stronger and had already taken her far enough from the resort that no one would hear her scream?

She didn't know, but she was going to make damned sure that whatever he was scheming didn't go off as planned.

Being careful not to move anything but her eyes, she scanned the space in which she now found herself.

The room was circular, with a heavy coating of dust on the floor and a few rotted furnishings leaning crookedly against the walls. There was a solid, rusted metal door next to the bed Eli was preparing that looked like it would take some serious strength to open and stairs leading up to a second floor that was shrouded in darkness. To her right were two mattresses lying limp on the floor—the source of the dirty hair and dried piss smell mixing with the general mustiness of the room, no doubt—and an almost artistic pyramid of beer bottles arranged in between them.

Beer bottles. Possible weapon.

Her mind registered the information, then estimated how long it would take her to reach the bottles, smash one into the concrete to create a jagged edge, and turn to meet her attacker.

Thirty seconds. Maybe less, but Eli was fast, he'd already proven that. He might reach her before she could prepare herself and then the element of surprise would be wasted. Even if she was ready for him, there was a chance he would be able to overpower her. He wasn't a big man, but she was still sluggish from whatever drug had been in his needle and not in the best physical condition.

She made a mental vow to hire a personal trainer as soon as they got back to the States, one as mean as Dom had been last summer, who would whip her back into fighting shape.

The next time she was in a situation like this, she wanted to know that her body was a loaded weapon, ready to fire.

And there would be a next time. She wasn't naïve enough to think all the darkness in her past was going to disappear if she escaped Eli and she wasn't going to die here tonight. She had babies at home who needed her and a husband who would be destroyed by a visit to a Samoan morgue to identify her body.

There won't be a visit to the morgue. Listen. Hear the waves?

What better place to dump an unwanted body?

With the tide going out until morning, you'll be swept so far out to sea your body will never be found.

Harley's tongue swept out to dampen her bone dry lips. She did hear the waves, but she wasn't going to sleep with the fishes tonight. Ignoring the voice of doom droning in her head, she let the sound of the waves crashing somewhere outside this building give her hope. She must not be too far from the resort, which meant help was close.

The old lighthouse! The one visible from the honeymoon suite. That had to be where he'd taken her. There wasn't another circular structure on the property and she sensed she hadn't been out long enough for Eli to drive her anywhere.

She glanced back at the heavy door. Eli had finished with the bed and was lighting candles. Time was running out.

She had to make a decision. Run? Or Fight?

If she ran, she had two choices—either make a break down the beach toward the honeymoon suite and hope Clay was there waiting for her, or run down the path leading through the dunes to the resort and pray someone was close enough to hear her scream before Eli caught up with her.

She wiggled her toes inside her high-heeled sandals. After years of art gallery openings and high-profile partying in her twenties, she was speedier in heels than most, but she would be faster barefoot.

Waiting until Eli bent to light another in a long line of candles, she reached down and tugged the ankle strap on one shoe and then the other, quietly slipping the leather through the buckle and sliding her feet free. Pulse pounding in her throat, she curled her fingers around the armrests of the chair and shifted her weight forward.

She would bolt in three, two…

Before she could reach one, the chair let out a soft squeak and Eli's head swiveled her way, his eyes opening wide when he saw that she was awake.

Shifting from flight to fight mode in an instant, she lunged to her right, grabbing two beer bottles from the top of the pile as Eli's footsteps slapped the floor behind her. As she spun to face him she lifted the bottles high, letting out a roar of outrage as she brought them down on his forehead with all the strength in her body, sending her attacker falling to his knees.

The crash as glass shattered against bone sent a painful vibration ricocheting up her arms all the way to her teeth, but she didn't let go of the bottle tops. She held tight, ready to ram the now jagged ends of the bottles into Eli's face when he came for her again.

But Eli didn't get up off of his knees.

Instead, he teetered there for a moment, his head lolling loosely on his shoulders, before falling onto his side in a heap.

Breath rushing out, Harley leaned over to see that his eyes were closed. That was all the confirmation she needed that it was time to run. Clinging tight to one bottle—just in case—she hurled the second to the ground, grabbed her heels in her free hand, and leapt over Eli's prone body. A soft voice in her head whispered that she should find Eli's gun and take it with her for protection, but she ignored it.

The man was out cold and she didn't want to risk getting close enough for him to grab her again. Even if he only stayed unconscious for a minute or two that would give her all the head start she needed to make it back to the resort. Back to Clay, who would know who to call to have a drug lord's lackey shipped to a jail in the States, even though the island nation of Samoa was one of the few countries without an extradition treaty with the U.S.

She hurried to the door, thinking of nothing but how much she needed Clay—

needed to see that he was all right, to feel his arms around her and to hear his voice assuring her that they were stronger than the people who wanted to hurt them. But the last thing she expected to see as she hauled open the heavy metal door amidst a squeak of rusty hinges, was Clay waiting for her on the other side, not ten feet from the entrance to the lighthouse.

CHAPTER TWELVE

Clay

*C*lay stumbled to a halt. The shock of seeing Harley burst out of the lighthouse in her bare feet, clutching a broken beer bottle, threw him for a second. The next second he shouted—

"Run, Harley! Go! Now! Call the police!"

He had no idea what she was doing here, but she had to go get help. If Stewart knew a witness was on her way to tell the authorities what she'd seen by the lighthouse, he might decide the risks of this plan suddenly outweighed the rewards.

Harley started to cut across the sand toward the hotel but lurched to a stop when she saw the man who stood behind him.

"Dad? Will?" Harley's shoes and the bottle in her other hand fell to the ground as her fingers fluttered to her throat. Even in the moonlight illuminating the dunes, turning everything beneath to alabaster and stone, he could see her skin go a shade paler. "Oh my God, Dad. What is this? What have you done? Give me my baby. Right now."

"It's not Will," Clay said, grunting as Stewart stepped closer, shoving the barrel of the gun into his back.

"Quiet, Hart, or I put a bullet through your spine," Stewart said before turning his attention back to Harley. "Of course this isn't Will, sweetheart. I would never put my grandchild's life in danger. But I do need you stay with me. No calling the police until we have a talk or I might have to hurt this sweet little girl."

"No. Don't even try that shit with me, Dad," Harley said, tears rising in her eyes as she shook her head. "Put the gun down. Whatever you were planning to do, it stops now. Let Clay go and give me the baby."

"I'm sorry, but I can't do that," Stewart said with an uncharacteristically nervous laugh. "I've lost everything. Everything I've worked and sacrificed for is crumbling into the sea and this is the only way to get it back."

"That's ridiculous. Put the gun down and talk to me for God's sake." Harley's eyes met Clay's, silently asking him if this was what she should be doing. He nodded almost imperceptibly, but it was clear she got the message loud and clear.

She refocused her attention on her father, dropping her voice as she took a small step forward, "Please, Dad. Talk to me. We can fix whatever's broken without anyone getting hurt. I know things have been ugly between us the past year, but they don't have to stay that way."

"No, they don't," Stewart agreed. "I should

have let you have Mallory. I see that now."

Clay's brow furrowed.

Mallory? Who the fuck was Mallory? And why didn't Harley seem surprised to hear the name?

"She doesn't matter anymore," Stewart continued. "Ian is dead and there is no evidence to tie me to what happened to the girl. She is nothing, less than nothing. But I let her ruin things between us before you were even discharged from the hospital last summer. I regret that, and I don't regret much."

"You don't like to let go. I know this about you." Harley sighed. "But it's not too late. Dom is in Georgia, near the cabin where Mallory was being held a few days ago. The man who has her can't have gotten far. Just tell me where they went and I can get Dom to—"

"I'm sorry," Stewart said, "but I can't tell you anything."

"Dad, please," Harley begged. "Have a little mercy for once in your life. The poor girl has been through enough."

Clay's jaw clenched. Clearly his wife had been keeping some secrets of her own. He just prayed they made it through this so he could find out what kind of trouble she'd gotten herself into this time.

"I would like to." Stewart's hard tone made it clear mercy was still a foreign concept. "But I don't know where Aaron took Mallory. All I know is that I'm ruined. Forever. No going back."

"Maybe that's a little melodramatic, Dad." Harley shifted another half step to her right. "Kind of like stealing someone's baby just to make a point in a family fight?"

"There's nothing overstated about this. Your husband and the criminal your sister married have destroyed an empire that took generations to build. There won't be a penny left after the crows finish picking at the carcass." Stewart pressed the gun into Clay's back until he winced at the pressure of metal against bone. "I hope you're pleased with yourself, Hart. Thanks to you, your sons will grow up paupers too ashamed to show their face in society."

Clay grunted in response, silently willing Stewart to hand the baby over to Harley. If the child was out of the way, Clay could disarm the older man in thirty seconds or less.

"I'm sorry, Dad, but that sounds crazy. What could Clay and Jackson have done to you?" Harley glanced over her shoulder at the door to the lighthouse, using the movement to edge farther to her right before she turned back to them with a frown. "Clay's retired and Jackson's been working as a bodyguard on an island in the middle of nowhere. They aren't exactly players in your kinds of games."

"Oh, they're players," Stewart said. "Players, schemers, liars, and thieves."

Clay had to literally bite his tongue to keep from responding. Harley was getting closer. Soon she'd be close enough to go for the baby if he went for the gun. And he instinctively knew that she would. As long as she was within arm's length, Harley wouldn't let that child hit the ground.

"They found the one thread that hadn't been tied," Stewart continued, his voice wavering. "It was years ago, not long after your mother left. I never drank before she left. But that night, I let my anger and pain get the better of me. I had half a bottle of scotch and got behind the wheel." He swallowed audibly. "I was driving too fast and the woman came out of nowhere. The roads were slick, but even if they hadn't been, there wasn't time to brake. I didn't even have time to try."

"Oh God, Dad," Harley muttered, glancing back at the lighthouse door again, making Clay wonder if there was a reason for it aside from using the tactic to get closer to her father.

Was there someone in there? Someone who was the reason Harley had burst through the door with a broken off bottle clutched in her hand?

"She was one of the people who camped out by the river year round, living in those rusted out trailers. She didn't have a tooth left in her head," Stewart continued as if that excused killing a woman while driving under the influence. "She would have been dead in a few years of malnutrition or drugs, anyway.

She wasn't worth losing everything. The sheriff understood. He took half a million and made it all go away. Until your husband and Jackson Hawke dug it all up again."

Harley's gaze shifted from her father to Clay. "Is that true, Clay?"

"Answer her, Hart," Stewart said. "Tell your wife what you've done."

"It's true." Clay held Harley's gaze, silently willing her to get closer to Stewart. "Jackson and I wanted to put your father away so he wouldn't be a danger to our families. We've been looking for something we could use to get a felony conviction for the past six months."

"You did that without telling me?" Harley's tone was outraged, but the step she took toward her father was calm, calculated. "Behind my back? Without even asking how I felt about my father going to jail for the rest of his life?"

"I did what I had to do. The kids are never going to be safe as long as he's free."

"Well, not now," Harley said, her volume rising. "Of course not now. You've pushed

Dad into a corner."

"Jesus, Harley." Clay allowed his own volume to rise, silently celebrating when the baby began to snuffle behind him. "You've got to be fucking kidding me!"

Harley stepped closer. "Well, how would you like it if someone made it their business to pull all your dirty laundry from the past few decades out into the light? I'm sure some of that wouldn't be very pretty, Clay."

"You can't possibly be on his side," Clay shouted, eyes darting hard to his left. They needed to make a move soon before Stewart realized they were playing him. "Are you listening to yourself?"

"Yes, I'm fucking listening," she said, eyes flying wide. "Now!"

Clay lifted his arm and Harley lunged under it as he spun, bringing the side of his palm down on Stewart's forearm, knocking the gun from his hand and tackling the older man to the ground. Before Clay's first blow connected, Harley was already rolling to the sand, the baby safe in her arms.

"You have the right to remain silent."

Clay wedged his knee in the middle of Stewart's back as he checked the rest of his pockets for weapons. "Anything you say can and will be used against you in a court of law."

"Damn you to hell," Stewart said, thrashing beneath him. "This isn't over. This isn't close to over."

"Clay," Harley said, moving to stand next to him, patting the back of the now wailing baby. "Clay, we need to talk."

He held up a finger. "You have the right to an attorney. If you cannot afford an attorney one will be appointed for you."

"Clay, seriously," Harley said.

"Do you understand these rights as they have been presented to you," Clay pushed on, determined to Mirandize the canny old bastard underneath him before he arranged for one-way transport back to the United States. Samoa might not have an extradition treaty, but as long as Clay handed Stewart off directly to the CIA, without the Samoan authorities getting involved, the entire diplomatic nightmare could be avoided and

Stewart would still end up behind bars where he belonged.

Clay was so focused on making sure Mason was read his rights and then restraining him using his belt as makeshift handcuffs, he didn't realize the door to the lighthouse had opened until Harley cursed and reached down to snatch Stewart's gun from the sand.

"Put the gun down, Eli." Harley angled her body, shielding the crying baby with her shoulders as she aimed the gun at the man who had just burst through the door, blood dripping down his face. "Don't give me an excuse to shoot you, because I will. It's been that kind of night."

Clay surged to his feet, planting a foot on Stewart to keep him down on the sand, fighting the urge to rush the man weaving back and forth on the path, a revolver clutched in the hand hanging by his side. He recognized that weasel face. This was one of the men who had taken Harley from their tent last year, who had intended to take turns raping her for his own amusement. Clay wanted to punch the bastard's face until he was bloodier than he was already, but he couldn't risk Eli getting off a shot before he took the other man down.

"I've got a gun, too." Eli sounded congested, no doubt from the dried blood filling his nose.

"You do," Harley said calmly. "But I've already got my gun aimed right at the center of your forehead and I'm a phenomenal shot. Aren't I, honey?"

"She is," Clay confirmed in an equally calm voice. "She really is. You're screwed, man. Might as well put the gun down and live to plead insanity."

"I'm not crazy." The man's dark eyes flicked from Harley to Clay and back again. "I'm trying to keep my promises, to finish what I started for Marlowe."

Clay shrugged one shoulder. "Can you keep promises to a dead man? What do you think, babe?"

"I think I would like to get this poor baby back to her mother and I'm tired of standing here talking to an idiot too stupid to understand that Marlowe never cared about anyone but himself," Harley snapped. "Put the gun down now, Eli, or I will shoot you and sleep like a baby tonight knowing you're too dead to fuck with me anymore."

Beneath his foot, Stewart grunted with laughter. "I told you she was my child."

"Shut up, Dad," Harley snapped. "Or I'll shoot you, too, and sleep even better." Her stone cold tone left no doubt that she meant every single word.

Uncertainty wavered across Eli's face. A moment later, he swallowed hard and let his gun fall to the sand.

"Smartest thing you've done all night," Harley said as Clay moved toward Eli to repeat the Miranda warning. He had no idea what country Eli was from, but Clay intended on shipping him back to the States with Stewart.

Maybe they could share a cell until the CIA got around to processing them.

He had just finished binding the man's hands behind his back—using Eli's belt this time—when his cell buzzed. He tugged it free, practically sagging with relief when he saw

Jackson's name on the screen.

"Perfect timing," he said with a heavy sigh. "How soon can you be at the old lighthouse on the Malolo resort?"

"Ten minutes," Jackson said. "I'm already on my way. Just got around the mountain and called as soon as I had service again. What's up? Hannah had a bad feeling that Harley was in trouble."

"We were both in trouble, but we're fine now," Clay said, shooting Harley an appraising look that made her mouth, "What?" The baby had quieted and she was obviously doing her best not to upset the child again while she bent down to strap her feet back into her shoes.

He held up a finger as he filled Jackson in. "I've got Stewart and one of Marlowe's goons tied up and in need of discreet transport to the airport. Preferably in the back of a windowless van to avoid any trouble with the Samoan authorities. It might be a few hours before I can get someone here to pick them up."

"The SUV has tinted windows," Jackson

said. "We can keep them bound and gagged in back. We'll figure out a way to get them out of the resort when I get there."

Clay thanked him and hung up, before leaning back against the lighthouse door, surveying the two captives face down in the sand. Finally, he let his gaze drift to his wife as he jabbed his thumb toward the building behind him. "So, anyone else in there that I should know about?"

She shook her head. "No, just him. But there's the wheelchair he used to bring me out here after he drugged me. We might be able to use that to get them both out to Jackson. If we make two trips."

She sighed, the last of her tough girl act fading away as her eyes filled with tears. "I'm so glad you're okay. I'm sorry I was keeping secrets."

"Me too," he said softly.

They moved at the same time, meeting in the middle for a hug hard enough to make the baby cry out and begin to fuss again.

"Sorry, sweet thing." Clay put a gentle hand on the baby's back as he bent to claim

LILI VALENTE

Harley's lips in a quick, hard, "we'll get through this, too" kiss. "You should take her back to the resort. Go to the front desk. Tell them you found her on the grounds near the garden, that someone must have left her there."

"I'll tell them the kiddie pool," Harley said, nodding as she backed away. "It's deserted over there. It would have taken a while for someone to hear her, even if she were crying at the top of her lungs."

"Perfect. I'll meet you back at the room when Jackson and I are finished."

"How about the lobby bar?" she asked, eyes shining. "And I'll have our things packed to leave? Call me crazy, but I'm not really in a party mood and I'd like to be there for Will's two a.m. feeding if possible. Just to hold him and know he's okay."

Clay nodded. "The lobby bar it is. Are you all right with being alone here for a few hours? You can come with us if you want. I thought you'd rather skip the rest of the drama, but—"

"You're right. I would. I'll be fine until you

get back," she said, a smile curving her lips. "Just stay safe, okay? That's what I need the most."

"Harley, don't go." Stewart flopped in the sand like a landed fish as he tried to turn to get a look at her. "Stay. Let me explain, I wasn't going to hurt anyone, I only wanted—"

"Oh, stuff a sock in it, Stewart." Harley scowled at her father, clinging tighter to the baby in her arms. "And don't bother sending any letters from prison. I don't have time for pen pals."

She turned to go, her hips swaying softly in her white dress, looking almost ghostly in the moonlight. The thought made Clay's chest clench as he dropped his head back to gaze up at the stars spinning overhead, grateful all the people he loved were still among the living.

CHAPTER THIRTEEN

Harley

By the time Clay returned to the hotel it was nearly two in the morning. It took another ten minutes for the sleepy valet to bring the rental car around to the lobby and Clay was forced to drive slowly on the poorly lit roads.

They kept the conversation light on the way back to Jackson and Hannah's, in silent agreement that the real things they needed to talk about were too big to tackle during a thirty-minute car ride. They pulled down the gravel drive to the house by the sea at a quarter 'til three, a full hour after Will's usual feeding time.

Harley had resigned herself to simply standing over Will's crib watching him sleep, but when they stepped into the house, Hannah was just settling onto the couch in the darkened living room with baby and bottle. She eagerly handed off both to her sister and sat close while Harley popped the bottle between Will's lips.

"I'm so glad you're okay," Hannah said. "I was scared to death for you. And I'm so not happy with Jackson or Clay right now. If they'd been honest with us, we could have both been more on guard. And maybe you would have seen trouble coming."

"I'm not really in a position to call people out about being honest," Harley said with a sigh. "I've been working on something for a while now. I should have told Clay—and you and Jackson, too—but I wanted to wait until I had good news to share."

Hannah turned her head, studying Harley out of the corners of her eyes. "Is this one of those secrets that's going to make me mad at you? If so, maybe wait and tell me tomorrow because my mad quota is about filled for tonight."

"No, I don't think it will make you mad at me." Harley wrinkled her nose. "At least not too mad. But it will certainly get you royally pissed at Dad."

Hannah waved a hand through the air. "Then go ahead and tell me, I couldn't be any more pissed at him than I am already."

Harley took a deep breath and filled Hannah in on the bare bones of the situation with Mallory, not surprised when her sister's jaw dropped and fire began to burn in her blue eyes.

"So Jackson and I have a nineteen-year-old half sister in common," Hannah said, blinking fast. "And Dad sold her to some creep who runs a human trafficking ring when she was a baby. And you and Dom have been searching for her for over a year, but Dad kept paying for the creep to move so this innocent girl is still a prisoner."

Gently, Harley tugged the nipple from the baby's mouth and turned him over her shoulder to burp him. "Yeah, that's about the size of it."

"I hope he gets the chair," Hannah said in a rare display of bloodthirstiness. "Or something slower and more painful." She stood, pacing away from the couch with her hands at the small of her back before spinning to face Harley. "I just can't believe it. The poor girl. I can't imagine what her life must have been like. Even if Dom finds her soon, how will she ever be okay? How can she lead a normal life or dream or love or believe she deserves happiness after everything she's been through?"

"I don't know." Harley watched her son's eyelids begin to droop as he slipped back into sleep, so grateful that she was still alive to ensure his life was as happy and peaceful as possible. "But we have to keep trying. And when we find her we need to show her that there are people in the world who are glad that she's around."

Hannah settled back on the couch, her hand on Harley's knee. "Of course we do. And we will. She can come live here with us if she wants. What's mine is hers."

Harley smiled. "You want to ask Jackson about that first? You guys are going to have a full house soon. A little bird told me twins were on the agenda."

Hannah's cheeks flushed. "Jackson or Clay?"

"Clay, on the way home." She glanced outside to the lanai, where Jackson and Clay both leaned against the deck railing, scotches in hand.

"Yes, well, twins or no twins, Jackson will want to help Mallory, too," Hannah said, lifting her chin. "And even if he didn't, he owes me one for lying to me for months. You heard that Dad sent a hit man after both Clay and Jackson, right? And that they got together and decided not to tell us a word about it?"

Harley's eyes went wide. "No, I didn't. When did this happen?"

"Right after Christmas," Hannah said. "So

for the past six months, they've been living a lie, pretending everything is fine while they secretly tried to put Daddy in jail."

Harley fought the urge to raise her voice. "What?"

Hannah nodded enthusiastically, clearly pleased to have someone to be outraged with. "Yes! And the excuse is that they didn't want to stress us out and put the babies in danger."

Harley cursed softly as she turned the now out-like-a-light Will over her shoulder to try to get one more burp out of the sleepy baby. "Well, at least it was a good reason. I mean, on the one hand, I understand why they did what they did. But on the other hand, I'm—"

"Mad as spit," Hannah supplied. "And not happy about being treated like a child. I mean, it's not like we both haven't been through things like this before. Maybe not while we were pregnant, but we know the Dad's Gone Crazy drill."

Harley's forehead smoothed as the implications of the past few hours hit full force. "But maybe never again," she said softly, afraid to say the words too loud and

ONE MORE SHAMELESS NIGHT

jinx them. "This might be the end of it, moo. Dad's going to jail. Most likely for the rest of his life."

Hannah pressed her lips together and nodded. "I know," she whispered. "I'm almost afraid to hope, but…maybe it's finally over. Maybe we get to be normal people from now on. Or close to it, anyway."

Normal. It reminded her of what Clay had said earlier tonight. That they might never be normal, but that he was still looking forward to a simpler life. Now the sentiment made much more sense.

What must it have been like for him? Hiding from her the fact that someone had tried to kill him and pretending everything was okay? It had to have been hard, painful, but he'd done it because he cared so much about her health and happiness.

As Clay turned to glance back through the windows, finding her eyes with a searching look, the last of her irritation faded away. They might have lied to each other, but both of their lies had come from a place of love and concern.

"Want me to put Will back to bed?" Hannah asked, nodding toward the window. "It looks like you two have some talking to do."

"That would be great." Harley leaned in to press a kiss to her sister's cheek. "Thank you for giving me a second chance. I'm so glad we're family again."

Hannah smiled as she shifted Will into her arms. "You've come a long way, you know. I'm proud of you. For what you've tried to do for Mallory. The old Harley wouldn't have cared that much."

"The old Harley would have cared," Harley said. "She would have just been too busy punishing people to devote much of her time to saving them."

"It's easier to be a hero when you know how much you're loved." Hannah stood and tilted her head toward the lanai. "Go talk to your husband. That way Jackson will be free to fight with me when I'm done with Will."

Harley grinned. "I like that you give him shit. He's so bossy."

"He is." Hannah winked. "But that's one of

the things I like best about him."

"Right." Harley cleared her throat. "I'm not going to touch that."

"Coward." Hannah laughed as she turned to cross the room, disappearing back into the nursery.

Harley watched until she closed the door behind her and then stood, ready to do whatever it took to avoid a fight. Since the day they'd said their vows, she and Clay had made it a point never to go to bed angry, and she didn't intend to start tonight.

CHAPTER FOURTEEN

Clay

*C*lay watched his wife step out onto the lanai—passing Jackson on his way back into the house—with a dozen different emotions swirling in his chest.

It had been a complicated, fraught, crazy, terrifying night. But right now everything felt very simple again. Harley and the kids were all safe and there was nothing on the agenda

159

tomorrow but to get as much sleep as possible, spend time floating in the ocean, and put this nightmare behind them.

"You want to walk down to the beach?" Harley reached out to take his hand cautiously in hers.

He shifted his grip, threading their fingers together and squeezing. "I do."

They headed down the stairs and across the patio, where the remnants of Hannah and Jasper's junk food fest was still littered across the outdoor table, then down a simple boardwalk across the dunes. At the end of the walkway, they slipped off their shoes and started across the sand toward the edge of the water. All around them, the beach glowed softly in the moonlight, like the surface of another planet where everything was muted and soft, with no dangerous corners or sharp edges.

"Hannah told me why you and Jackson were trying to put my father in jail," Harley said, pausing to hold up a foot and let sand filter through her toes. "I know we still have a lot to talk about, but I want you to know that

I understand why you made the decision you did."

"I just wanted you to feel safe," Clay said, swinging their joined arms. "And happy. It happened right when you were finally feeling better and enjoying the pregnancy. I didn't want to take that away from you."

"I understand. And that's the same reason I didn't tell you that Dom and I were looking for Mallory."

"Right. Mallory." Clay stopped at the edge of where the dry sand met the beach recently kissed by the tide. "I gathered that she's one of your father's victims, but—"

"She's my sister. Well, my half sister," Harley said, before launching into an explanation so fantastical it would have been unbelievable in any other family.

But thanks to the unrepentant selfishness and evil of their patriarch, the story of an infant sold into slavery to punish her parents for having an affair was just the latest installment in the Mason family insanity.

"When Dad found out I was looking for her, he wasn't happy," Harley continued. "He threatened Jasper, saying he would take a 'child for a child' if I didn't back off."

"Jesus." Clay blinked, his brow furrowed tight. *"Take* as in kidnap? Or something worse?"

"I don't know." Harley shook her head. "I didn't think he would have hurt Jasper, but I couldn't know for sure." She looked up at him, pushing the hair the sea breeze had whipped into her eyes away from her face. "But I couldn't stop trying to free Mallory. I just couldn't, no matter what the risks. And since you had a security detail following me and Jasper, when he was at school, I knew he was being watched like a hawk, so it didn't seem—"

"You knew?" Clay asked, making a mental note to fire whoever had let himself be made.

"Of course, I did." Harley laughed beneath her breath. "I mean, I only caught a glimpse of them once or twice, but you don't spend half your life on the run and not know when you're being followed. They were clearly CIA types, though, so I wasn't worried."

She stepped closer, looping her arms

around his waist. "In fact, I thought it was sweet. You're a very thoughtful paranoid person."

"Turns out I wasn't paranoid enough." Clay pulled her closer, loving the feel of her, safe and warm against him. "I should have brought security with us. And I never should have let you leave the table alone tonight."

"If you'd tried to go with me I would have thought you were crazy," she said. "I still would. We can't let one terrible night make us live in fear, especially when everything turned out okay. I even got my phone and purse back. Someone found them by the kiddie pool and turned them in to the front desk."

"A Good Samaritan, huh? We needed one of them tonight."

"And we got one." She tipped her head coyly to one side. "Besides, how am I going to sneak around to call people behind your back if you're always with me?"

"Right. People. People like Dom." His breath rushed out. "I'm not even going to ask if anything but business is going on between you two."

"Good." Harley nodded. "And thank you. If you *had* asked, then I would have had to get angry with you and I'm running low on outrage energy. You should know by now there is no one but you. Never has been, never will be."

"I do know that." Clay tilted his forehead closer to hers. "But I am going to ask if we can both be more honest with each other from here on out? And that's not an idle question. Do you think that's possible for us? Or are we always going to make excuses to keep secrets?"

"I…don't know." Harley's hands smoothed up his sides to lie flat on his chest, right above where his heart beat beneath his ribs. "But I do know that I love you and I trust you and that we're an amazing team."

"We are," he agreed, thinking of how seamlessly they'd played off of each other by the lighthouse. "Again, I have to reiterate that you would have been an amazing spy."

"And I have to reiterate that I have no interest in following the rules long enough to become qualified to do something like that."

She grinned, but her expression sobered as she added, "But I do want to be on your team for a long, long time. I'm willing to work on the secrets thing."

She lifted her shoulder and let it fall. "It's just hard when my gut is screaming that the best thing I can do for you is *not* tell you things that are going to upset you for no reason. I mean, what's the point when there's absolutely nothing you can do to make them better?"

"In this situation, I have to disagree with your assessment," he said, pressing on before she could argue with him. "But I did have a lot on my plate. Knowing Stewart was threatening Jasper might have been enough to tip me over into an...unhealthy frame of mind."

Harley searched his face, nodding slowly when she saw the scary truth he didn't bother to hide. "I understand. I would have felt the same way if I knew he'd tried to have you killed. So maybe it was best that we shared the load. Even if we didn't know we were sharing it."

Clay's lips curved. "So basically, you're saying the honesty project is doomed before it even starts?"

"No, I'm saying that we're good together and we need to trust that. Even if we don't do marriage the way most people do it." Her arms slid up to link behind his neck as she smiled. "But I was serious when I said I would give it a try and I'll start right now. While I was hanging out in the lobby waiting for you, I arranged to have the swing dismantled, boxed up, and sent via airmail. It will be waiting for us when we get home."

"You didn't have to do that. I know you weren't thrilled about it."

"But I will be." She leaned closer, her breasts flattening against his chest, reminding him that they hadn't gotten a chance for round two, let alone three or four. "Tonight I was reminded that life is too short not to let yourself get strapped into a bondage swing. Even if you do look a little gremlin-ish under your clothes."

He laughed. "You are not the least bit gremlin-ish."

"I know. I'm irresistible," she said with a wink. "Or, at least, this one guy said I was. This one time."

"I think I remember that time," he said, beginning to bunch her skirt up in his hands. "But I might need a little something to refresh my memory."

"Right now?" she asked, a wicked gleam sparkling to life in her eyes. "On the beach?"

"Why do you think I led you all the way down here to the water," he said, slipping his hand beneath the elastic band of her panties to cup her ass, "where they can't see us from the house?"

"But we'll get sand in uncomfortable places," she said, even as she let him slide her panties down her thighs and stepped out of them. Taking her back into his arms, he lay down on the cool ground and pulled her on top.

"I love sand in uncomfortable places." He lifted his hips, granting her easier access as she went to work on his belt buckle. "It gets me hot."

"You're a strange man, Mr. Hart." She

finished with his zipper, biting her lip as she freed his already rock hard cock from his boxer briefs. "But clearly you tell the truth. Sand in your ass *does* get you hot."

"Or it could be knowing you're not wearing any panties," he said, "and that I'm going to be inside you soon."

"Very soon," she said, summoning a groan from deep in his throat as she lifted her skirt, holding it in the air while he fit himself to her opening. And then, inch by agonizing, beautiful inch she dropped her hips, encasing him in her heat.

"Is it still crazy beautiful?" She held his gaze as they rocked together, slow and deep, the way they both liked it best when she was on top. "One year later?"

"Always." He cupped her face, pulling her down for a kiss before promising against her lips, "Always and forever, and then a little bit extra because you're too good to let go after just one lifetime."

"Ditto, my love," she whispered.

And as the moon slipped behind the mountain and the first hint of the coming sun began to lighten the horizon, they welcomed the start of their second year as a family, knowing it would be as crazy beautiful as the first.

And keep reading for a sneak peek of Lili's first standalone contemporary romance, MAGNIFICENT BASTARD! Out now.

by Lili Valente

F*ck Prince Charming. Sometimes, you need a Magnificent Bastard.

Face it, ladies: love sucks and then you cry…while your ex rides off into the sunset banging your best friend.

But why let a break-up end in tears when it can end with sweet revenge? Enter Magnificent Bastard Consulting and me, chief executive bastard. I've got it all—looks, brains, a heart of gold, and the killer instinct guaran-damn-teed to make your ex regret the day he said goodbye.

With the help of my virtual assistant, I've built an empire giving broken-hearted women the vengeance they deserve, while keeping myself far from the front lines of the heart. Life is a bowl of cherries, until my *virtual* assistant shows up on my *real* doorstep for the first

time, begging for a Magnificent Bastard
intervention of her own.

Damn... She's a bona fide sex kitten.

I pride myself on being a true pro, but
pretending to be her lover soon leads to
giving it to her good, hard, fast, and up against
the wall. And somewhere between getting
balls deep in my sweet and sexy assistant and
watching her ex beg for a second chance, I
break every last one of my damn rules—
professional *and* personal.

So what's my next move? Fight for the girl
who makes me want to get up on a white
horse and ride to her rescue, or stay a
Magnificent Bastard to the end?

Warning: MAGNIFICENT BASTARD is a
stand-alone erotic romance told from the
hero's point of view. No cliffhanger. Lots of
dirty talk.

Prologue

Picture this: it's a rainy spring day in the city. The streets are covered in a fine layer of mud and soggy garbage, the sun is a distant memory from another, brighter time, when you were still stupid enough to believe in happy endings, and you've just been dumped so hard your heart looks like it's gone three rounds with Mike Tyson.

You're ugly crying in a corner with a box of wine and a chocolate bar the size of your forearm, wishing Prince Charming would come scoop you up on his white horse and carry you far away from all those nasty memories of Mr. Wrong, but I'm here to tell you, ladies—

You need to stop that shit.

Stop it. Right now.

Why? Because Prince Charming is a crock of shit. He doesn't exist and even if he did, he's a fucking wimp.

When you're down and out and your heart has been ripped to shreds by an asshole with a dickish-side a mile wide, you don't need Prince Charming. You need a man who's not afraid to get his hands dirty, a man who can teach Mr. Wrong a thing or two about what it feels like to be deceived, betrayed, and laid low by the one person in the world you thought you could trust. What you need is a Magnificent Bastard, your very own one-man vengeance machine.

Love isn't a fairy tale, sweetheart; it's war, and now you've got a soldier with an anti-asshole missile on your side.

Want to ruin your ex's reputation? No

problem. Every true asshole has a few skeletons in his closet and I specialize in making skeletons dance out of the darkness and into the light. Want to send that fucker to jail? A little harder, but often still possible. I only accept cases involving the very worst examples of mankind, the most miserable liars and cheats and scoundrels. Those types tend to be good at covering their tracks, but I've delivered exes locked in police cuffs before.

Want to make your former lover green with envy? Make him wish he'd never kicked you off the love wagon, spat in your face, and walked away? Well, that, cupcake…that's what I'm best at.

I've been blessed with a face that turns heads, worked hard for a body that inspires shudders of lust at twenty paces, and honed my envy-inspiring skills into a razor sharp weapon I wield with ruthless efficiency. I will make you feel like a queen and ensure your ex doesn't miss a minute of it. You'll be treated like an irreplaceable treasure, pampered like a princess, and kissed like a slut who can't get enough of my magnificent dick.

In reality, of course, things between us will never go further than a kiss, but your ex won't know that. He'll see your flushed cheeks, lust-glazed eyes, and wobbly legs and think I'm giving it to you hard every night.

He'll imagine my hands on your ass, my fingers slipping between your legs, and your pussy slick and dripping just for me. He'll imagine you screaming my name while you ride my cock and remember all the times he was lucky enough to be balls deep in your incomparable snatch. Before long, he'll have a jealousy hard-on so bad he'll come crawling back to you on his belly, begging for a second chance.

But you won't give it to him.

Did you hear that?

Even so, it bears repeating—

You. Will not. Give that fucking loser a second chance.

By the time I'm through with you, you will know deep down in the marrow of your bones that you're better than that. You'll understand that you deserve a man whose eyes won't wander, whose hands won't hurt, and whose heart belongs to you and only you. By the end of our time together, you will be able to look down at the sniveling, pathetic, limp-dicked excuse for a man you used to love and tell him that he has no power over you.

Not anymore. You will be free to move on with your life without any of the ugly, bad breakup, psychic baggage.

And that, gorgeous, is the most important

of the services I deliver. I give you back to *you*, the only person who can be trusted to steer your course as you ride off into the sunset.

But if for some reason, you break this all-important rule. If you sour the gift you've been given by going back to Major Dickweed, don't bother contacting me again. No amount of money will convince me to pick up the phone.

A Magnificent Bastard intervention is a once in a lifetime opportunity. One and done, no exceptions.

None.

Not even for her, the woman who made me break all my other rules, the woman who made me think—for one amazing week—that even magnificent bastards can live happily ever after.

Magnificent Bastard is out now!

Acknowledgements

First and foremost, thank you to my readers. Every email and post on my Facebook page have meant so much. I can't express how deeply grateful I am for the chance to entertain you.

More big thanks to my Street Team, who I am convinced are the sweetest, funniest, kindest group of people around. You inspire me and keep me going and I'm not sure I'd be one-third as productive without you. Big tackle hugs to all.

More thanks to Kara H. for organizational excellence and helping me get the word out. (No one would have heard of the books without you!) Thanks to the Facebook groups who have welcomed me in, to the bloggers who have taken a chance on a newbie, and to everyone who has taken time out of their day to write and post a review.

And of course, many thanks to my husband, who not only loves me well but also supports me in everything I do. I don't know how I got so lucky, man, but I am hanging on tight to you.

Tell Lili your favorite part!

I love reading your thoughts about the books and your review matters. Reviews help readers find new-to-them authors to enjoy. So if you could take a moment to leave a review letting me know your favorite part of the story—nothing fancy required, even a sentence or two would be wonderful—I would be deeply grateful.

About the Author

Lili Valente has slept under the stars in Greece, eaten dinner at midnight with French men who couldn't be trusted to keep their mouths on their food, and walked alone through Munich's red light district after dark and lived to tell the tale.

These days you can find her writing in a tent beside the sea, drinking coconut water and thinking delightfully dirty thoughts.

Lili loves to hear from her readers. You can reach her via email at lili.valente.romance@gmail.com or like her page on Facebook https://www.facebook.com/AuthorLiliValent e?ref=hl

You can also visit her website: http://www.lilivalente.com/

Also By Lili Valente

Sexy Flirty Dirty Series:

Magnificent Bastard (A Sexy Standalone

Romantic Comedy)

Spectacular Rascal (A Sexy Standalone

Romantic Comedy)

The Under His Command Series:

Controlling Her Pleasure

Commanding Her Trust

Claiming Her Heart

The Bought by the Billionaire Series:

Dark Domination

Deep Domination

Desperate Domination

Divine Domination

The Kidnapped by the Billionaire Series:

Dirty Twisted Love

Filthy Wicked Love

Crazy Beautiful Love

One More Shameless Night

The Bedding the Bad Boy Series:

The Bad Boy's Temptation

The Bad Boy's Seduction

The Bad Boy's Redemption